IsleWrite...twentythirty

© IsleWrite 2020

twentythirty selection
© IsleWrite

Individual contributions
© The contributors

Each contributor has asserted his or her right to be identified as the author of his or her work

All rights reserved

Published by IsleWrite, Thanet, Kent

A CIP catalogue record of this book is available from the British Library

ISBN 9781838058203

Design
Graeme Campbell
graemecampbell.design

Print
En Route Design & Print Ltd
en-route.co.uk

What a humbling honour it is to write the foreword for this glorious prose and verse.

IsleWrite - a dedicated community of writers - speak to us about childhood, relationships, friendships and love, about birth and mortality, about where we came from and where we are, with a combination of fearless experiment and rich tradition. I've had the privilege of seeing some of these writers start their journey, scribbling early ideas around a workshopping table; I've seen their work fly out into the world, in publications, on a stage, set to music; they are writing their own truth, and sharing it with us.

These are the stories and poems that connect us as people, and in these strange times, that connection is precious. I hope you enjoy this collection.

<u>Dr Roopa Farooki</u>

Dr Roopa Farooki is the award-winning author of six literary novels for adults that have been published in over twenty countries, and has been listed for the Women's Prize for Fiction three times.

She received an Arts Council Award and Authors' Foundation Prize for work that increases understanding between cultures. She has lectured in Prose Fiction at Canterbury Christchurch University, in the English faculty at the University of Kent, and she currently lectures on the Masters in Creative Writing at the University of Oxford.

Roopa is an NHS junior doctor, a Royal Literary Fund Fellow for Kent, and has a new series for children published by Oxford University Press.

Welcome to twentythirty

It's been my privilege to curate and present
twentythirty this collection of work by thirty writers
celebrating twenty years of *IsleWrite*. The pieces
– many commercially successful or award-winning –
represent a small part of the wide-ranging subjects
and styles produced over the years by the prolific
and ever-developing group.

I am indebted to Patricia Mahoney for her
painstaking editorial contribution to the process.

Jill Anabona Smith *Editor*

Annie Watson

Annie was born in Galway, Ireland, lived in London most of her adult life and moved to Broadstairs in 2012. She enjoys writing about her life as a secretary in the 1970s when letters were dictated by male (usually) bosses, noted using shorthand and then typed on manual typewriters. She is an admirer of the short story genre, particularly by Irish writers and has made several efforts to replicate it encouraged by her IsleWrite colleagues. Most recently, her short story *Holiday in Galway* was published in the Ramsgate Festival of Sound 2019 publication *Time Flies*.

Annie has travelled in Africa, Asia and other parts of the world and sometimes the people she met and their experiences find a way into her writing.

Reconciliation

Charlie has to think for a moment about where he parked the car, then walks down the cobbled street towards the river Lee. Michael follows a few paces behind.

There's a fierce chill in the air – you wouldn't want to be walking far says Michael, pulling his collar up.

Charlie unlocks the Volvo Estate, slips into the driver's seat and unlocks the passenger door.

A great car for the country, Charlie, I wouldn't mind one myself but it'll be a few years yet 'til I get my licence back.

Charlie knows the road to Bandon well, turning left at the now-derelict ballroom.

Didn't we have some great times inside there says Michael, or out by the back wall. You'd pretend it was to look at the moon and stars but the girls knew it wasn't romance we were after.

Would you ever shut up for a while, Michael, I'm still trying to take in the news. It's a big shock for a man to find out he has a grandchild he didn't know about.

Sorry Charlie but he's a little dote and Fiona will be relieved her father wants to see her again. It was a terrible thing for her to bring disgrace to the family and be banished to England for an abortion.

I never wanted that for her, Michael, it was her mother's idea and Eileen arranged everything. I only wrote the cheque.

A shame Eileen didn't survive long enough to find out what Fiona had done says Michael. That cancer kills you quick if it's the wrong kind.

Yes definitely the wrong kind, thinks Charlie, although he can't help musing on how his life has changed for the better since she'd passed away. Women seemed to find a well-groomed widower an attractive proposition and he's never shied away from a little flirtation.

This is Fiona's house, Charlie. Pull up on the left and I'll tell her you're here.

Charlie sees a swing in the front garden and an abandoned football. He says a silent prayer that she's forgiven him as he steps out of the car.

Fiona emerges holding a small boy in a green tracksuit by the hand. Say hello to your Grandad Charlie, Declan. You two have some catching up to do.

Louis Brothnias

Louis has no particular genre and writes short stories about whatever may inspire him at the time. He also develops concepts and offers an alternative interpretation of commonly held views. He often does not accept the 'explanations' provided preferring to write his own script. He believes too many questions remain unasked so no answer is then required.

Ice Cold Finale

Ever since my first day at Infants' school Raymond had latched on to me. I never knew what I had done to be the focus of his attention, but he hardly ever let me alone. I was terrified of Raymond. He bullied and tormented me, body-whipping me with a water-soaked rolled-up towel.

I learned later that he had 'verbally abused' me too. I did not understand what that meant or then know how to explain it, but that's what he did and I could never tell anyone. I became timid and withdrawn. Any confidence I once had was seriously damaged and there was not much left by the time I went on to Junior school. A scared little boy and nobody knew why.

Several years later I discovered contact sports. Rugby was my baptism of fire. Tough and a great game. I felt very comfortable in this environment and it was hardly surprising that I should raise the level to the one-on-one combat sports of boxing and martial arts. I became a very capable fighter, yet without a violent nature. Perhaps it's self-confidence that determines the difference between assertiveness and just being aggressive.

In my middle age, I was running through a local park as part of my regular training regime. It was lightly snowing. Near the middle of the park, surrounded by trees was a small lake that had frozen over. My balaclava, gloves and winter running clothes kept me warm while I sweated from the result of my exertions but I was used to outdoor sport in the winter.

I passed a lone man exercising his dog off the lead. Suddenly the dog ran onto the ice and the man screamed 'Come back, boy'. I stopped and turned towards the unpleasant sounding tone. The man was walking over towards the nervous-looking animal as it stood still on the ice. As he approached, the dog ran off leaving the man standing on the frozen lake near the bank. He was a heavy man and the inevitable happened. The ice cracked under his weight and he began to sink into the freezing cold water beneath, gasping in surprise.

I instinctively ran towards the bank. Maybe I could get hold of him and pull him out, though I'd consciously decided I wouldn't venture onto the ice. There was nobody else about that I could see. Even the dog seemed to have deserted his master. The two of us were absolutely alone. I had to do something. By the time I reached the frozen-water's edge, the man had managed to pull himself clear and was reaching out and scrabbling for a hold on the snow-covered bank.

I looked down into his face.

Raymond.

It was possible that his shock and my balaclava may have conspired to hide my identity. He didn't know who I was. All my early school-day terrors returned and transformed into rage as the memories flooded into my mind. In a moment of unthinking madness I kicked Raymond's head – hard - as he struggled to stand. This single blow must have rendered him momentarily unconscious as he released his grip on the snow-covered bank. He slipped back into the freezing water this time disappearing completely under the ice.

I never saw Raymond again, though I did retrieve the dog's lead that had been dropped.

I wondered how long in advance it was necessary to define premeditation in first-degree murder. A day? A week? A month? In my case it was nearly forty years. I knew in a flash when I saw it was Raymond trying to reach the bank that I had wanted him dead for all that time. Still, was it premeditation or manslaughter maybe with diminished responsibility? I didn't care. Raymond was dead.

Three weeks later all the ice had disappeared and Raymond's body, bloated and putrefying, was found. From the bruise on his left temple it was concluded at the inquest that he had lost his footing and struck the ice with his head. The ice had cracked, his body had slipped through into the freezing water and he had drowned.

Nobody had missed Raymond. No explanation could be offered to explain his being on the ice and it was supposed he had lost his way during a snowstorm. A verdict of accidental death was returned, but I knew differently.

I had possibly managed to get away with murder and I felt not the slightest sense of guilt though I was not particularly proud of what I had done - killing a defenseless man - but I was at last free of those childhood terrors. The bully had at last met with his, very much delayed, comeuppance.

I stroked my newly adopted dog, Raymond, with the very foot that had dispatched his previous owner. I told my friends that my dog was a stray I'd found roaming in the terribly cold weather and they thought it very generous of me to give the animal a new home. As he contentedly lay on the floor in front of me I smiled, confident that my damaged soul had finally been fully repaired.

LOUIS' WORK IS PUBLISHED ONLINE AND IN ANTHOLOGIES *CREATIVEACRE.CO.UK*

Lynne Gardiner

Lynne joined IsleWrite after winning a competition set by them to write a story in fifty words. Her work has appeared regularly in anthologies since then. She lives in Margate and Grenada, West Indies.

The Merman

Bridget slid a large file of newspapers from the high shelf and checked its contents carefully for the catalogue she was preparing. She was alone in the Museum that day but perfectly at peace in the small room which used to be a cell, part of the old Police Station building. Its thick walls kept the space cool and quiet, the hubbub of the busy square outside barely audible. As part of her Archivist course she had been given the job of sorting out this room which had been forgotten for many years, making some sense of all the clutter dumped in here over time.

She had just found several heavy bound volumes of local newspapers, the pages yellow and mottled and she breathed in the musty air with satisfaction - something about old newsprint she just loved. She knew most people found her obsession with the past rather odd but she was quite content, doing what she enjoyed.

She had already made some progress around the room but she was cramped for space and struggled to put the volume of newspapers back in place, it kept catching on something. Standing on tiptoe she reached her hand into the cobwebby recess as far as she could, her fingertips scrabbling at something hard stuck at the back. Slowly she edged it forward until it was near enough for her to reach. A wooden box a little larger than a shoebox tied together tightly with string fell into her arms.

She brushed off the dust with a cloth turning the box over for any indication of what it might contain but found nothing. The knots securing the box were impregnable so placing the box on the floor she found her scissors and cut them through.

The lid bounced off with a sigh revealing something wrapped in newspaper underneath. Kneeling down, she gently peeled back the covering.

'Jesus!' She gasped in horror, falling backwards into a pile of books, knocking the box over with her foot, its contents spilling out onto the floor.

A mummified face stared back at her, tight shut eyes over a rictus grin, its small boy-like body tapering to a spiny fin. A cardboard label fluttered nearby and taking a deep breath Bridget reached for it.

Merman? Dreamland circa 1920's? was scrawled in pencil.

Of course, she thought, heart still pounding, the Freak Show - bearded ladies, midgets, Siamese twins and the like. She had heard about these so-called mermen before - tests on examples had shown they were a mixture of papier-mâché and fish skin. Gathering herself she reached for her phone and positioned herself to take a photo of the creature.

Suddenly she heard a door slam behind her.

'Bridget, it's only me,' came the cheery voice of John Hedge, the Curator, come to lock up.

She took the photo quickly and instinctively covered the Merman and put the box back over it.

'Don't tell him' whispered in her head.

Gathering her belongings, she backed out of the cell shutting the door behind her. Lowering her head she ignored John's chatter as best she could and left quickly, she needed to get home.

Back in her small rented room she made herself a sandwich and trawled the internet for references to mermen which seemed to confirm what she already knew and had images of known fakes. She

. . >

opened her phone to compare her creature but annoyingly, the photo appeared blank except for a strange glow in the middle of the image. She downloaded it onto the laptop for a better view. Zooming onto the glow, two blue eyes stared back at her from a black screen.

By the time she awoke the next day after a restless night and technicolour dreams, Bridget had realised she was just being foolish. The Merman was simply a sham, made up of old bits and pieces to fool a gullible public and the photo was just a mis-shot. As she ate her breakfast she decided that today she would do her job, record and catalogue it for the Museum. John Hedge would be thrilled.

Nothing had changed in the cell since she had closed the door the night before and she knelt down to remove the box and paper covering the creature. Picking it up she looked more critically at it, her repulsion held at bay by logic. It did look very life-like, a small shrunken head with sparse, brittle hair and tiny claw-like hands reaching out from a brown leathery body transmuting into a sorry-looking single scaly fin.

With a duster she carefully began to clean, cosseting it in her lap. She damped the cloth with her water bottle and stroked it over the dull and grimy tail which soon began to gleam, shimmering with all the colours of the sea. Suddenly she felt a small movement like a gasp of breath and she jolted with pain - the Merman had hold of her thumb, his needle-like fingers piercing her skin.

'Free me' rang like a bell in her head as she screamed and dropped the creature

She ran out to the bathroom, holding her bloody thumb under the tap, her heart hammering. She sat on the bathroom floor, trying to calm down and make sense of it all. There was no mistaking the pin pricks in her thumb but could she have just snarled herself on it by accident?

There was a sound of whistling from the corridor and the heavy tread of John Hedge. She heard him call her name and went slowly out to find him.

He was standing in her cell with the Merman in his hands.

'Where on earth did you find this?' he grinned, 'what a gem, this is just what we need for our Dreamland exhibition, it'll bring in the crowds - they love this sort of thing. Hideous isn't it?'

Bridget nodded politely and listened to his chatter watching nervously as he tossed the Merman from hand to hand.

'Let me take it,' she said eventually, 'it's quite fragile and I was in the middle of cleaning it.'

He left her to it promising to be back later and Bridget sat with the Merman in her lap suddenly feeling very sad that she would play a part in putting it back on public display as a freak of nature once more. A tear fell from her eye and splashed on its chest. She felt its little heart beat.

Wrapping it carefully in her jumper and cradling it like a baby Bridget left the Museum and made her way towards the seafront. A heavy drizzle was in the air and the beach deserted except for a few hardy folk. Seagulls squawked noisily around and she gripped him tightly to her, stumbling across the clinging sand. She headed to the lido, slipping off her shoes and making her way along its edge, glassy with algae, to the far end. The sea was just beginning to slip over the top of the lido and her feet were cold and wet but she lowered herself down until she was sitting on the wall itself.

She unwrapped the Merman. He glowed, hair the colour of seaweed, skin like polished shell, tail shot through with iridescence and his eyes the deepest blue. She lowered him into the welcoming waves and watched as he swam away.

'Not hideous at all,' she murmured, 'it's the most beautiful thing I've ever seen.'

. . /

Sally Allen

Sally has been telling stories since she was about six/seven years old, when she made up tales to amuse her younger brother.

At junior school she progressed to telling stories to her class, left in charge when her teachers needed to be elsewhere. This proved very popular with her classmates, and she was known as 'the girl with the lively imagination'.

In 2012, Sally was a member of a small group in Suffolk that published online an experimental collaborative novel, *Strange and Familiar Consequences*, each member of the group writing one chapter apiece.

She has been a contributing member of IsleWrite for about five years.

The meeting

It was starting to rain again as I ran across the road to the church hall. I could see that lights were already on inside. My stomach was in knots, I was so nervous, but I knew that this had to be faced - things had gone too far this time.

There were about 17 or 18 people in the hall, sitting in a circle on plastic chairs, with just two vacant seats. They all looked up when I came in. I did a quick sweep of the circle: equal numbers, men and women, mixed ages/backgrounds, three non-Caucasians.

An overweight, bearded man stood up and gestured for me to take a seat. He was wearing a jumper with possibly the most pulled threads I had ever seen. I found it hard not to stare.

He spoke. 'Welcome, everyone. Thank you for turning out on such a dismal evening. Tonight, as you will see, we have a newcomer in our midst.' He pointed vaguely in my direction so everyone looked at me again. My stomach churned. 'Perhaps you would like to say something about yourself, and why you are here tonight?' he smiled at me.

I stood up, knees knocking, hands sweating. 'Hello, my name is Suze, and I'm a chocoholic.'

There was a soft murmur of 'Hello, Suze' and a general nodding of heads from the group.

'And I'm here tonight,' I continued, a lump now starting to form in my throat, 'because yesterday I was arrested for shoplifting... from Thorntons... three boxes of Continental Selection.'

There was a shuffling of chairs and something like a rumble of human thunder running through the group. And then they all applauded. I wasn't expecting that and sat down, searching in my pocket for a dry paper handkerchief to wipe my eyes.

But the group was buzzing:
'Oh, the praline…'
'I love the truffles'
'The alpini are to die for!'
'And that fudge, *so* velvety.'

A Nigerian lady I knew from the greengrocer's shop whispered, 'Mmm, I just *Love* those rum truffles.'

The man next to her said, 'There ain't no rum truffles in the Continental!'

Across the circle a person I recognised from the post office called out, 'Oh yes there are, you daft sod!'

The Rastafarian sitting opposite winked at me and said, in a broad Welsh accent, 'Look, see what you've started,' and then roared with laughter, slapping his hands on his knees.

By now there was chattering coming from all quarters and the meeting was in chaos.

Beardy-bloke stood up, cleared his throat. 'Thank you, Suze, for sharing that with us. It was very brave, and we can all sympathise with your pain. Now if we can hear from someone else…'

A painfully thin girl, pale-faced, with dark circles under her eyes, had started to rock back and forth, wailing 'I want a Yorkie bar. I *need* a Yorkie. Please someone get me a Yorkie.' The older woman next to her tried to comfort her, but the girl lashed out, knocking the woman's spectacles to the floor. The girl's wailing continued.

'Hey, there's no need for that,' said Beardy-bloke, trying to break up the ensuing scuffle, but ending up on the floor instead.

Two other people now weighed in to help, but Beardy thought he was being attacked and he hit out, too.

The place had descended into mayhem when a rather sour-faced vicar pulled a monster-size Toblerone from his backpack and, using it as a cudgel, started laying into the wrangling assembly.

Everyone stopped and stared open-mouthed at the vicar. They started moving towards him, slowly, like a pack circling its prey. He backed away, hugging the fractured Toblerone to his chest, but they were too wily for him, and finally they wrenched it free, so many eager fingers shredding the wrapping and tearing chunks off to cram into salivating mouths.

I got my coat and left, more shaken than when I'd arrived.

Laure Meloy

Laure is an award-winning opera singer, having sung with companies around the world, including Royal Opera House Covent Garden, Hungarian State Opera and the Metropolitan Opera in New York. As a writer, she collaborated on the script of an opera/cabaret called *One Art* (which she also performed), publishes a blog about life in the arts, and is currently working on both a career memoir and a family history. This is her first published short story.

Venezuela

Would you like a ride home after the rehearsal?

Well, I was just going to take the subway.

Don't bother with that, save a token - my car is parked nearby. You're on the Upper West Side, right?

Yeah - 93rd between West End and Riverside.

I'm at 82nd and Columbus. Totally not out of my way. C'mon!

Okay, thanks.

This the first time you've sung with the Bronx Opera?

No, actually I was in *L'Elisir* last season. You?

Oh I did a couple of shows a few years back,

just after I graduated. Before I got married.

Right. That would've been before I moved to New York, so -

Yeah, my husband didn't mind me singing, but his family are really old fashioned. I mean, they're a bit weird about me doing this now, but I told them I had to do something. I was going stir crazy...
This is mine. Get in.

Nice car...
You're brave driving in the city. I gave up my car when I moved here. It must be impossible to find parking spaces.

Well, my building has a garage in the basement. But, yeah, when I go places in the city. You get used to it.

Wow. You have a car phone. I've never even seen one of those before. Must be expensive.

My in-laws pay for that. They insist. You know, in case I'm out with the baby and something happens. Ever since... Look, you probably heard, my husband died a few months ago.

Oh my god. No, I... I'm so sorry. That must be hard. And you have a baby? Wow...

Yeah, it's pretty awful.

So your in-laws... do they help out a lot?

Well yes and no. They look after us financially, so I can afford to stay in our apartment and keep this car and everything. But they don't live here, so it's not like they can babysit all the time.

Right.

I have a nanny for that anyway. They live in Venezuela. He was from Venezuela, my husband.

Oh. So...

They're a really close family. He worked in the family business. They can't understand me wanting a career in opera. They thought I was giving it up when we got married and then when the baby came along. But I was always going to go back to it. You know what I mean?

Of course. I'd be the same. God, it's your career, right?

Yeah, his family don't really get it, though. It's kind of like, well, I suppose it's partly just they're a bit traditional about women and all that. Like I say, close knit and everybody works for the family firm...

Still, you need an outlet, right? It must be kind of therapeutic... sorry - not my business.

No, it's fine. You're right, it is.

For what it's worth, I think you're doing the right thing. You sing really well. It would be a shame to just give it up.

Thanks.

I guess I just assumed everyone else in the cast was a starving artist, you know, working temp jobs and hoping they get noticed in this little production. I guess you never know... well, I mean, you're really brave.

Yeah. Thanks.

Sorry, I guess you might not want to talk about it -

No, it's fine. Really.

I was married. No kids, though. Divorced now... well, technically a dissolution. Just couldn't manage the long distance thing...

Oh. Sorry.

No big deal. A bit sad, but... I mean, not dramatic, you know, just drifted apart -

He was killed.

Sorry?

My husband. He was killed. I'm not supposed to talk about it. It wasn't an accident.

Woah. Oh my god. I'm so sorry -

I'm not supposed to talk about it. Venezuela, you know? I mean, you know what I mean?

Er. Well...

I just had to tell someone. Say it out loud. Don't say anything.

Yeah. I, uh... I won't. Of course not. Who would I tell? No, of course not...
Look, are you OK? I'm fine to just listen, you know? No judgment.
Are you going to be OK?

Fine. Sorry, there's this guy - been tailgating me...
Please forget what I said. I don't know what I'm talking about. Just getting stressed about the show.
Look, we're here.

What?

This is your block, right?

Oh, yeah.

Great. OK. I'll just let you out here.

Oh... OK. Thanks. See you at the next rehearsal then.

Gotta go. That guy behind me is getting pissed off. Sorry.

Bye...

The Bribe

Rumours that one of us is a spy have been circulating the office for some time. No one is sure who it is, or brave enough to discuss it openly. It's 1946 and I've worked in Moscow at the Ministry of State Security the longest and am used to gossip. We're a team of twelve, including one woman, Varinka.

We've been told to assemble in the committee room to have our photograph taken. Yuri, who is taking the photo, places Varinka near the centre.

"Now all smile" encourages Yuri, "think of our wonderful Russia." He adjusts the lens, looks at us with an exaggerated wide grin and clicks the shutter button.

Is this all a ruse to catch the perpetrator? Since working here, this is the first time we've had a team photograph taken. Is the photo needed to disclose the identity of the informant? I glance furtively at Luka, he looks uncomfortable. Until now, I've never seen Misha smile. It all feels... wrong. Is this all a subterfuge? All this is going through my mind, while someone takes Yuri's place, so he can be in a photo. This feels utterly incongruous. A slightly theatrical and fabricated atmosphere shrouds the place. They don't seem convincing enough to me. Have they been rehearsing? Being an extremely perceptive person, experience has taught me to listen to my gut feelings.

Why are they surreptitiously glancing at me? I'm feeling nervous. All my instincts tell me something is about to happen. Perhaps it is... to

Tricia Brady

Tricia started writing eight years ago. Since then she has had three short stories published and won several prizes including having a story broadcast twice on BBC Radio Kent. This gave her the confidence to join a writing group and she's been a member of IsleWrite for six years and says their constructive criticism, camaraderie and encouragement has been a great help.

Her genre varies but the stories all have one thing in common... a twist at the end.

me. Beads of sweat form on my forehead. Acutely aware of all my senses, I now resent ever taking that bribe. Casually, reaching behind my lapel I ease out the fatal capsule. Standard issue to a double agent.

The door opposite me opens, everyone turns to look at a young man entering the room. No one is looking in my direction, so casually I put the capsule into my mouth. He is walking towards me looking down, as if worried about what he is holding. The staff are blocking my view. I can't see his gun pointing towards me, but I can visualise it.

At training school, we had three rules; one, rely on your instincts; two, confide in no one; and three, don't get caught. Biting hard on the capsule releases the fatal cyanide which trickles down and burns my throat. Not wanting to be tortured or spend the rest of my life as a prisoner in brutal gulags, or internment camps, this is my only option.

My legs give way and I collapse to the floor, like a marionette puppet that has had its strings cut. Unaware of my predicament, everyone parts and reveals the lad carrying a cake and bottles of vodka precariously bulging out of his pockets. A banner reads 'With Best Wishes' held up by the now relaxed and laughing group.

I hear a huge gasp as Varinka rushes to my aid. She drops down onto her knees beside me. I can't talk, my tongue feels like a piece of lead in my mouth but I can hear.

"Quick comrades, help, he's fainted, we must revive him!" she shouts. "We want him to enjoy his surprise birthday party."

Jan de Swarte

Jan was born in rural mid Wales of Welsh parents. Aged fifteen she moved to Cornwall for A levels at Penzance Grammar School where an inspirational and renowned English teacher, Miss Tranter, encouraged her to write daily - advice she has followed.

Leaving school Jan studied French at the Sorbonne, then taught English in Madrid. Back in England, she trained as a nurse, later obtaining an Arts Degree in London. Following a move to Broadstairs, in 2012 she joined IsleWrite whose support she has been grateful for.

Christmas Conundrum

Sitting at her kitchen table enjoying a guilty post-prandial cigarette, her thoughts wandered. Was this allowed, Nancy considered? Smoking in your own home?

Probably not, the way things were going. Here she took an extravagant pull on her cigarette, inhaling deeply.

After all, she justified, it's only an occasional treat, a reward for hard work - she'd been to the gym that morning and shopped for her unwell neighbour - but what would Melanie, her lovely, dutiful, social worker daughter say? Mel, who was the teeniest bit judgemental about what she called 'wickedly selfish bad habits'?

Nancy giggled a tad nervously and took another pull at her cigarette coughing a bit as she did.

The sudden trilling of the telephone was like an electric shock causing her to shoot out of her chair, hastily stubbing out her half-smoked cigarette and upending on the floor her other guilty pleasure, the glass of Beaujolais.

Ruefully surveying the shattered glass, Nancy reached for the phone with a plaintive 'Hello?'

'Mum, is that you? You sound a bit weary.'

'Hello Mel - you can deduce all that from a hello?'

'How are you Mum? How's the arthritis?'

'Not too bad m'dear - but how are all of you? That little grandson of mine - doing all right at school?'

'He's fine. So am I. So's Johnny. The thing is Ma, I want to talk about Christmas.'

'Christmas! But Mel it's only just October.'

'I know, but I wanted to let you know early so that we can make some plans. Johnny, Max and I have been invited to the States for a couple of weeks over Christmas to stay with Diana, Johnny's sister. It's their silver wedding and it's going to be a big family gathering - and, oh Mum, it's the first Christmas where we've all got the same holiday time. Johnny is owed a ton of time-off and must take it before the New Year. But I'm worried about you being on your own. I'm going to try and make brother Bob do the honours for once...'

'Oh don't, Mel. He needs his free time too and I shan't mind at all. You deserve a lovely long break.'

Nancy was experiencing a feeling of pure joy. How heavenly to have a long quiet time to herself. No frenzied perpetual cooking, cleaning, bed making, unmaking. She could make plans - even go away. No, she didn't want Bob, much as she loved him, for Christmas, nor his lazy, overweight wife, nor the two boisterous boys - not when the promise of a stress-free holiday was on offer.

'Mum, are you there? We'll cancel if you can't manage.'

'You'll do no such thing. I'll be fine. I'll miss you of course, but you don't live so very far that we can't do our celebrations another time. And I have good neighbours.'

'Well if you're sure - we'll book the flights early. Talk later. Bye Mum.'

Nancy set to work picking up the shards of glass from her wine-stained matting, her thoughts whirling as she digested Melanie's news. She continued to feel pleasurably excited.

Forty years of doing Christmas and though she'd loved it when the children were small she felt she'd done her bit.

Abroad perhaps? All those places she'd loved when she was young. Florence, Rome, Venice. Or better still, Vienna. Salzburg for some wonderful Mozart concerts. Or perhaps, her excitement mounted, she'd go to the northern countries. Iceland, Norway. See the Northern lights. The possibilities were endless.

Her fantasies were interrupted by the shrill ringing of the phone again.

'Hi mum, it's Bob. Just been on the phone to Mel. Look here, no way are you going to be on your own this Christmas. Jen and the boys and I will all come down. We'll get a nice big tree that the kids can decorate, bring a ton of food. We so look forward to your lovely cooking - Jen's not much cop in that direction as you know.

So get out the diary Mum. Circle the 23rd of December to at least the 6th January.'

A CHRISTMAS CONUNDRUM WAS FIRST PUBLISHED IN WINTER WORDS, THE ISLEWRITE 2016 ANTHOLOGY

City living

There's something lonely about the black taxi,
Its orange light glowing a blur
Through the drizzle of the dark city streets
On a Saturday at midnight.
The solitary drunk tells his story
And then vomits all over the back seat.
Just trying to survive like the rest of us,
The drunk and the driver.

Rita Hardwick

Rita started writing at an early age and briefly joined a writing group when in Sheffield. She has completed a powerfully disturbing novel about surviving domestic abuse and is one of the newest members of IsleWrite, coming to her first meeting at the Broadstairs Library in 2019.

There's something lonely about the baby rat
Scuttling behind the plant pots,
Disappearing through the gap in the wall
To find shelter under my sink.
It seeks the comfort of its nesting place
Leaving behind the rancid stench of germs.
Just trying to survive like the rest of us,
The scared rat and the plants.

There's something lonely about the passing years,
The way the kids play between
Metal bars framing identical flats,
Knowing the Council owns it all.
Youths struggle their way up and leave behind
Grandmas in aprons clutching aching joints.
Just trying to survive like the rest of us,
The young and old alike.

Maria Brown

After a career in the Royal Air Force, Maria gained a PhD in History of Art from the University of Kent at Canterbury and went on to tutor first year students.

On taking early retirement Maria wrote articles and reviews for arts magazines and, encouraged by a group of like-minded friends, discovered a love for creative writing culminating in winning first prize in a Kent Libraries Short Story Competition.

The Smack Boy

Let me introduce myself. George Edward Ellis, born in Hastings when Queen Victoria was an old lady. Orphan, smack boy, fisherman, boat owner.

My mother was Romany; I never knew her but I've only got to look in the mirror to see the connection I have with her race. Dark curls, blue eyes, square jaw. Some say handsome but I don't know about that. I'm tall and strong thank God, that's what's allowed me to survive a hard life.

My father was the eldest son of wealthy saw mill owners who disowned him on his marriage. After my mother died, they offered to have him back but not us, my brother and sister and me; spawn of a suspect race we were sent to orphanages. I don't know where my siblings ended up but at six years of age I arrived at the Gordon Boys Home in Dover. They weren't cruel to us but they weren't very kind either; we were fed and educated and at fourteen sent out into the world as apprentices to a trade.

As my fourteenth birthday approached I began to wonder what plans had been made for me. I gathered my courage and approached the Matron.

'Ellis, yes I think we have managed to place you,' she said, her starched apron and bonnet crackling with indignation at being spoken to without invitation. 'You're to be an indentured apprentice to Mr Smith at Ramsgate, Master of one of the fishing smacks in the harbour there. That means, George Ellis, that you are legally bound to him for five years. You must agree to serve your Master faithfully, not absent yourself from service or frequent alehouses or taverns. Do you understand?'

I nodded.

'In return your Master agrees to teach you the business and provide you with meat and drink while at sea only. When you're on shore you'll be paid a penny a day as cook and, on promotion to deck boy, you'll get a silver sixpence.' Did I read some softening of her strong features as she looked at me? 'You must learn to fend for yourself George but you may be offered lodging with your Master on shore. Otherwise you'll have to live in the Smack Boys Home.'

Thus my future was mapped out for me.

When I arrived in Ramsgate, my few belongings carefully folded into a small bag, fishing was the main industry; I'd been told there were as many as 168 smacks registered here. The spectacular sight of their ochre sails filled the harbour with a curtain of crimson, mirroring the evening sun as it set behind Smeaton's lighthouse. It was

IMAGE - THE RAMSGATE HOME FOR SMACK BOYS © GRAEME CAMPBELL

. . >

all new to me then but repairing those red sails with cold, chapped hands was to become part of my life while on shore.

I was to be housed with many other boys in the Smack Boys Home, next to the Sailors' Church facing the harbour. The Master and Matron, Mr and Mrs Taylor were waiting to show me round. On the ground floor was a mess room, offices, storerooms and lockers for our clothes while upstairs there was a washroom and individual bunks for 58 of us.

'This home is probably the only one in the country.' Mr Taylor informed me. 'It's not a bad lodging for an orphan. Before it was built the smack boys, some younger than you, had nowhere to go and were running wild through the town, terrorising the inhabitants. There was

a lot of stealing and half the apprentices ended up in prison.'

'In return you are to keep everything here clean and tidy,' Mrs Taylor chipped in. 'I won't have any rowdy behaviour or swearing.'

'I'm Ernie,' announced a small tousle-haired chap occupying the next bunk. 'What's your name?'

'George Ellis.'

'Been to sea before then?'

I shook my head, gathering up my belongings. I was well used to holding on tightly to my meagre possessions.

'You got a few surprises in store mate.'

He offered me a sweet – that was the first surprise. In the orphanage what was yours was fiercely held on to, nobody gave anything away, it was too hard to come by.

'You must be the one going to Ginger Smith on Veda. He ain't bad, you'll be all right with him. Wallop your knuckles with sticks some of them, or chuck icy water over you for nothing. Last winter one of my mates was put overboard and towed for ten minutes for answering back. Nearly killed him but who was there to care?'

At dawn a huge man with fiery red hair was waiting for me on the dockside. 'Come on board son,' he said gruffly, 'I'll show you round, no time to waste - we've got to catch the tide. You'll start off as cook. There's four of us to feed and you're to see to all the meals. We're usually away about eight to ten days and we bring all the food we need with us.'

He led me into the tiny galley where there was a small, coal-burning stove. An upright boiler with an open fire was over the top.

'You put the vegetables in those nets over there and drop them into the boiler. Beef is cooked in the beef kettle and the fish we catch is fried and served with fried sea-biscuits – just knock the weevils out first. You don't get any pay while we're at sea, but you can eat as much as you like, we don't go hungry. And you're entitled to a share in any salvage, small fish, dog fish and crabs which you can sell when we get back to shore.' With that he left me to it.

'Are you seasick?' he called down the hatchway.

'I don't know Sir'.

He snorted in amusement. 'We'll soon find out. Once we're off the Westards you can start by cooking some fish for breakfast. Don't look so worried, you'll get used to it boy.'

And he was right I did.

When I came back from the Great War, I found waiting for me a small amount of money – it seemed a lot to me then. From my father I was told. Conscience money. Enough to buy a couple of steam trawlers *The Mills*. What else did I know?

In 1935, *The Mill 'O' Buckie* was savaged by ferocious gales off Rosslare and limped home, three weeks late with her masts smashed and nets gone. A local paper of Thursday 31st January 1935 reported:

The drifter trawler 'Mill 'O' Buckie' ran aground during the severe gale on Friday night off Rosslare on the Irish coast. Despite the vessel's precarious position, the skipper and crew gallantly stuck to the ship, and on two occasions refused to leave in response to offers of help from ashore where their peril was observed. Fortunately the vessel held her ground.

Nobody was getting their hands on my possession and taking her for salvage. I told you before I never gave anything away without a fight.

IMAGE - SMACK BOYS LOCKERS © JILL ANABONA SMITH

. . /

Nancy Charley

Nancy lives in Ashford, working part-time in London as the Archivist for the Royal Asiatic Society.

The Gospel of Trickster was published in May 2019 by *Hercules Editions* and Nancy's been touring a performance of the collection. Presciently another collection from Smokestack Books called *How Death Came into the World* was published in 2020.

A Song of Hibernation

I wrapped my heart in a cotton shroud,
I wound my heart in a silk cocoon,
I gave my heart to the carrion crows,
who flew my heart to a lace day moon.

The moon sank into a bruise-tinged haze,
my heart slipped into the cold cold waves.
The current twisting from flow to ebb
carried my heart away away.

I trapped my sorrow behind panes of glass,
I hid my body in a pinewood shed,
I pooled my tears for marygold drink,
I stifled my sobs in spider webs.

But a money-spinner comforted me,
crawled my hand as I scrawled my hurt,
taught my lament to the screaming gulls,
scattered my anguish to pecking culvers.

I will bathe my face in the morning dew,
I will pinch off fear to feed crane flies,
I will sprinkle self-pity along the shingle,
skimming pebbles as anger dives.

My skin will absorb a radiant sunset,
my body will bask in crepuscular rays,
I will wade in the shallows when cats' paws thrill,
I will dance to the moon's corona display.

My heart will return when autumn is dead,
once winter is sifted and spring has sprung,
my heart will stir in its shrouding cocoon,
bloody my body, release my tongue.

My heart will return as a cormorant
lumbering silently over the sea,
oiled and preened and cruciate,
embracing others and saving me.

A SONG OF HIBERNATION IS FROM NANCY CHARLEY'S COLLECTION, *LITTLE BLUE HUT* (SMOKESTACK BOOKS 2017). NANCY CAN BE CONTACTED ON NANCYCHARLEY@HOTMAIL.COM

Alison Boots

Alison has been a writer most of her life and has worked as a professional musician in duos and bands throughout Europe. She has been awarded a BA (Hons) in Creative Writing and is currently working on her first major work, a thriller set in contemporary Berlin. She lists *Doctor Who* and *World of Warcraft* among her favourite hobbies.

Seeing is Believing

'You're fat, you're fat, you've gone to seed.'

Tessa's pounding feet labour the point as she skirts the clump of elder and turns sharp right up the path to the cliff top. There is something immensely satisfying about stamping through puddles, feeling the mud slapping up bare leg, especially when you're cross.

She glances up. There is the man, silhouetted against the sky, his dog by his side. Once again she wishes she had the nerve to stop and pass the time of day, dare to face him directly. Cool as ice in the summer heat, he is standing by the bench, his golden retriever at his side, gazing out to sea as if keeping a vigil for someone far away.

He never moves or speaks, standing there with his fingertips just touching the dog's head, and the tenderness of that one gesture tugs at the lonely place in her heart with a deep pang.

On her way up the hill she can observe him freely, taking in his fine, sensitive features and the way the dark hair sweeps away from his face in the wind. Only his appalling dress sense mars the dramatic effect of man and dog against the sky. Black jeans, brown shoes, odd socks, pale blue jumper, startlingly orange jacket, all of which remind her of Martin's worst jibe of all, when he compared her to a stuffed olive in a jar of jellied eels.

• • •

Tessa had honestly loved Martin, and she had believed he loved her. Perhaps, for a while, he had, but nothing she did ever seemed right. When her mum had her accident and Tessa decided to go down to the coast to look after her, Martin was furious.

'Who's going to look after me while you're away?' he demanded.

'It's only a couple of weeks. I'm sure you can manage,' said Tessa. 'Order takeaways if you don't want to cook.'

But a series of texts from Martin followed Tessa on the long drive to the coast: how did the washing machine work, what day did the bins go out, why hadn't she ironed his shirts before she left?

Mum recovered quickly, and the texts dried up, but Martin remained distant and uninterested whenever Tessa phoned him.

'You must go home,' Mum had urged Tessa after one particularly awkward call. 'Surprise him. Make a nice meal, sit down together, talk it out.'

So Tessa drove home with a boot full of Martin's favourite foods and a bottle of prosecco, only to find him watching a box set on their sofa, lying back in the arms of someone called Freida.

At first he had apologised. Then he got defensive and blurted out that Tessa was going to seed, blaming her for being fat, uninteresting, boring and going nowhere. Well she did go somewhere, straight back to her car and Mum's retirement bungalow on the coast.

It was the best decision of her life.

She found a good job at the local primary, a rented cottage by the harbour, new friends. But two years on she still felt raw. It was proving a long, hard road to run Martin out of her head and out of her life.

Every now and then he would phone, like he had this morning. 'Can we talk?' he asked, all bright and perky as if they had only spoken yesterday.

'Well,' she replied, 'I certainly haven't lost the power of speech in the last two years.'

'I just –' Martin said, 'I wondered how you are.'

'Fine.'

He seemed surprised at her tone. 'Are you still angry at me?'

'I've moved on, Martin.'

'You haven't got someone else, have you?'

'As if it's any business of yours!' she snapped.

He paused, then added, 'Freida and I split up.' Another pause. 'I really miss you Tessa. I still love you.'

'No you don't,' she bit back. 'You just need someone to iron your shirts.'

Then before he could start ranting at her for their breakup and ending with the accusation that she had let herself go and was fat, fat, fat, she had slammed down the receiver and headed out for her run.

• • •

Tessa has grown to love this little seaside town with its art gallery, its coffee shops and its quiet air of optimism. Now Martin's call has brought back all the misery and made her feel useless again.

As she struggles up the hill towards man and dog, her resolve to stop and speak to him fails again and she looks away. Yesterday his dog's nose just touched her hand as she passed. Cold, wet, gone in a second, it was as if she had momentarily touched another world.

But today, just as she draws level with him, the man says suddenly, 'Lovely morning, isn't it?'

Caught off-guard, her foot snags on a tussock and she falls, hitting the ground with a heavy thump and an involuntary grunt. She tries to roll over, leap up, carry on, and can't, winded. Tears of self-pity well in her eyes. She wipes them away angrily. Why doesn't he come to her aid? Is he laughing at her? Worse, is he sneering?

. . >

She chances a glance at him. He has taken a couple of steps, leaning forward, both hands outstretched, seeking. 'Where are you? Are you all right?'

Oh, why is she so unobservant? He's blind. It's obvious, from the mismatched clothes, his frailty, to the uncertainty in his reaching hands. She feels dumber than ever.

'Over here. Yes, I'm all right,' she calls, relieved he can't see her red sweaty face. She reaches out and as their hands clasp her impression of frailty evaporates. His grip is strong and certain as he pulls her upright and he doesn't release her but draws her close, his other hand resting on her shoulder, a gesture of strength and comfort. The dog is beside him, pressing between them.

'Get off Jimbo,' he says amiably, adding, 'he's worried you're hurt.'

'Only my dignity,' Tessa says, bravely ignoring her grazed knee and gorse prickled thigh. 'I should look where I'm going.'

'It's my fault. I distracted you, but I couldn't let another day go by without speaking to you.'

'I didn't realise you're blind,' she admits. 'I feel such an idiot. I'm sorry, I just – thought you weren't interested.' Then she carries on in a rush. 'Which wouldn't surprise me, the way I look. I'm trying to lose weight and get fit.'

'You felt light as a feather when I pulled you up,' he says with a smile. 'And you must be pretty fit to run up that hill every day.'

He takes her elbow, guides her to the seat and they sit down. Jimbo brings him a stick, lays it across his knees. He throws it, the dog races away, tail waving like a flag, ears flapping.

'I look a mess,' Tessa mutters, dabbing her cut knee with a tissue.

'I doubt that,' he says. His voice is deep, with a slight Welsh lilt. Jimbo returns with the stick, he throws it again. 'I can tell by your step that you're heavy of heart, not heavy in body. I can tell by your choice of perfume that you are gentle, and kind. Most importantly, Jimbo likes you, for a thrill of excitement runs through him as you pass by. I'm Owen. And you are?'

'Tessa,' she says, and adds, quoting Martin, 'as broad in the beam as a Cross Channel Ferry.'

When he smiles, it's like the sun coming out. 'I'm sure that's rubbish. May I?' His hands find her face and feather over her cheek, her neck, her shoulders, to her waist, a gentle inquisition that is personal without being intimate. He feels the undried tears on her cheeks and the smile she can't keep from her lips and his face is intense in concentration.

'You have clear, soft skin, your hair is like curled silk and your shape is firm, not flabby. But you are far too hot, and your pulse is racing.' With a shake of his head he gives that utterly disconcerting smile again. 'You do know, don't you, that overdoing the jogging is as bad for you as not doing it at all?'

'I need to get fit,' she insists.

'A brisk walk is just as good,' he says. 'And far more pleasurable. You have time to notice things; the smell of the earth, the sound of the sea. Lonely blind men hanging about hoping you will say good morning.'

'I didn't quite have the courage,' Tessa says, adding, 'Have you always been blind?'

'IED. Afghanistan. Four years ago.' His eyes, unseeing, gaze outwards over the sea. 'I work at the lifeboat station now, fielding emergency calls on the radio. You?'

'When my ex, Martin and I, split up, I moved down here. It's near my mother, and I have a job teaching at the primary, and a little cottage by the harbour.'

'Aha,' he exclaims. 'I've placed you now, the new teacher. My niece Rosie is at the primary.'

That familiar Welsh lilt. 'Ah yes,' she says, making the connection with one of her favourite pupils. 'She's mentioned her Uncle Owen a couple of times.'

'She's a tyke, that one,' he says with a chuckle. 'Delights in moving stuff around my house so I can't find it.'

'You live alone?' she asks, more hopefully than she would like to admit.

'Just me and Jimbo at the moment. There's a fearsome woman who comes in to clean, 'cos that's the one thing I can't do myself. Terrifies me, she does.'

Tessa can't imagine him being scared of anyone; he seems so solid, so self-possessed.

The dog returns to his side. Feeling with his hands Owen takes the stick and they spend five minutes in a tug of war, Jimbo grunting with the effort, tail wagging, but unable to free the stick. When Owen lets go suddenly Jimbo jerks back, then lays the stick back on his lap.

'More tomorrow, boyo.'

With deft hands he picks up the dog's harness, fastens it on. 'Will you take a brisk walk with me back down the hill? To get off some of that non-existent fat you insist you have?'

They stand up, he offers her his arm. She takes it.

'I fear I would be a sad disappointment if you could see me,' she says as they set out. 'All sweaty and covered in mud.'

'I can live happily with my illusion,' he says. 'What illusion is your ex living with these days?'

As they walk arm in arm down the hill she pours out the whole sorry tale.

'Saying you're fat,' he says, 'is just the excuse Martin used to make himself feel better for his appalling behaviour.'

'If I'm not fat, you can't be blind,' she responds.

'I can see some light and shade, and some outlines,' he says. 'I'm working on a technique of feeling colours through my fingers. I think I might be getting the hang of it.'

She glances at the extraordinary clash of colours he is wearing, decides not to tell him. Not yet, anyway. He might just have terrible dress sense. Or maybe Rosie has been rearranging his wardrobe.

She takes a deep breath, takes the plunge. 'There's a café on the sea front where they serve a very decent cup of coffee and an utterly indecent bacon sandwich,' she suggests. 'What do you think?'

'What would Martin say?' Owen asks. He looks her way, and she notices how expressive his face is, his quizzical expression, the humour around the corners of his mouth.

'I don't care,' she says, suddenly realising that at last it's true, she doesn't care. 'It's my life, I'll do what I like!'

'Brilliant,' he says tightening his grip on her arm. 'Bacon it is. And extra slices on the side for Jimbo.'

Together they walk down the hill. Not that briskly, but companionably; their steps perfectly in time.

SEEING IS BELIEVING FIRST PUBLISHED IN *PEOPLE'S FRIEND* IN 2019

../

Fi McKinlay

Fi is a writer, poet,
facilitator, mentor,
coach and business
change agent.

The Friendship Circle

Bonds so tight they cannot be broken Always loose enough to welcome Abundance in every form Flows from expanding hearts Time passes as our lives are lived Paths like roots entwine and grow Laughter and tears, fun and tears, Such care brimming with love But when the friendship circle comes together It is as if the dance never stopped had never began But is never ending

Mary Glass

Mary is (she says) the least likely of the IsleWrite group to be nominated for an OBE for services to literature, her only claim to fame being the publication of one short story in a women's magazine in the year 2002, for which she was paid a princely sum equivalent to one week's old age pension at that time.

At the age now of 87 (nearer 88) and in the middle of her third unpublished novel, she feels it unlikely that she will ever win a Booker Prize, so scribbles short tales which she hopes her now teenage grandchildren will read one day if they can drag themselves away from their iPads and mobile phones.

Seven

It's the school holidays. I'm in the supermarket with the twins, Doran and Tianna.

They're seven now, becoming helpful little people, putting my shopping from the trolley on to the checkout belt, then helping me stow it into shopping bags while chatting with the lady on the till. They're all innocence and curiosity, their lives full of gadgets and modern technology.

For me, seven was an age when I discovered that not everyone lived in a town, in a street of shops - behind one of them - with no garden to play in, no trees; that some people actually washed every morning in an upstairs bathroom and not in an ancient kitchen sink on the ground floor. But what you've never had you never miss and until I was their age and learned about the wider world I'd been quite happy with my rather restricted existence.

It was the 3rd of September, towards the end of the summer holidays in 1939 and my parents and I went to visit Aunt Rose who lived in the country at Shorne, between Rochester and Gravesend, not too many miles away. She was my mother's older sister and I was to stay with her. The family had decided her home would be much safer than living as we did behind the shop just five minutes from the Dockyard which they were certain would be a target in the war that began that very day.

Aunt's house was a modern semi, with hot and cold running water, a garden back and front and an apple orchard next door, another across the road and only half a dozen houses in sight.

I would walk up narrow lanes between fields to get to the village school which, instead of a concrete playground, had a grassy area with shady trees behind which one could hide from playmates.

For a few idyllic months, there were lazy

days when I played ball in the garden with Sandy, Aunty's 57-varieties dog or strolled along the road with Aunt Rose to buy whipped cream walnuts, our favourites, in the quaint little shop. There was only one small counter displaying mainly sweets and cigarettes and from time to time the owner would run outside to serve petrol from the village's only pump.

Alas, it was not to last. All too soon my parents discovered three things.

Because of the number of evacuees in the school I was not getting nearly as much education as they thought I should. My old headmaster Mr Llewellyn kindly sent me work to do when my mother told him she was worried I was not being given classes every day at the school in Shorne.

Secondly, Herr Hitler didn't seem to be aiming too often for the Dockyard and finally, in spite of being in the countryside, Aunty's house wasn't as safe as they'd anticipated, being on a flight path to London.

So soon I was back in the town, and the street full of shops and my old school, sadly now depleted of staff and pupils. My best friend Chrissie was no longer here. She'd been evacuated to Wales and would be there until the war ended.

Even home was different. My parents moved our beds from the first floor into the cellar and we slept there every night. But I soon settled into the new town routine and didn't, at that time, hanker for a country life.

I enjoyed school and before I knew

it, the 1940 summer holidays were approaching. Sorting out who would or wouldn't go up a class, Mr Llewellyn called a group of us into his room and asked our ages.

'I don't want to know how old you'll be next year, but how old you are today,' he said firmly.

'I'm seven,' I said when it was my turn, 'but I'll be eight the day after tomorrow,' I dared to add. I didn't want to get left behind in my present class by just two days.

And that is how, as opposed to other years of my childhood, I remember seven so clearly. I never forgot my few months in the country and all my adult life have thought how nice it would be to live in a little village. Alas I've never done so – one has to go where the work is - and now, of course, that I'm well beyond having to worry about work I have the good sense to realise that life in a village nowadays is probably not what it was then.

But I do wonder if my little twins, when they're in their dotage, will remember seven or any other special childhood year. What will the world be like at the end of the twenty-first century? Will there be any countryside left in England by then?

I hope that whatever state the world is in, Doran and Tianna will look back to a time long ago when they too had happy schooldays and sometimes helped Granny with her shopping in a funny old place called a supermarket.

June Angliss

June started writing a Sci-Fi novel in 1976. As a member of Havering Writers Circle she came second in an over 60's writing competition, had a story published online for *Indian Women Writers 4WI*, a short story published in an Indian children's magazine and a Christmas story published in *Weekly News*. In 2009 she moved to Broadstairs, joined IsleWrite and became an active member contributing regularly to its anthologies and promoting its work in the community. In 2014, June collaborated with the late Hilary McBride on a collection of short stories *Exactly the same but oh so different!* Her work has been published in numerous anthologies including *Time Flies* as part of the 2019 Ramsgate Festival of Sound.

She recently returned to her novel and its prescient themes.

Ellington House

It is such a wonderful day today here at Ellington House. The weather is exceedingly clement and the six dogs are enjoying themselves chasing squirrels.

I take a stroll along the terrace and through the grounds, amazed at the number of people around me. Many seem to be having picnics on our lawns but I do not remember anyone asking permission. Mind, they seem to be reasonably well-behaved and the dogs do not seem inclined to interfere so I assume all is well.

Many of these people must belong to a group of mummers as they all appear to be unusually dressed. I shall look forward to their entertaining me later in the day. I expect it is a surprise from my husband, Adam Sprackling, although of late he has been greatly bad-tempered and when he is in the house is to be avoided at all costs.

HERE LYETH BVRIED Y BODY OF St ADAM SPRAKELING
K SONNE TO RObt SPRAKELING GENT. LEAVING ISSVE 7
SONNES RObt SPRAKELING: ADAM SPRAKELING: IOHN
SPRAKELING: HENRY SPRAKELING: HENRY SPRAKELING:
CHARLES SPRAKELING: THOMAS SPRAKELING: AND 10
DAVGHTERS NAMED IVDETH SPRAKELING: ELIZABETH
SPRAKELING: KATHEREN SPRAKELING: MARY
SPRAKELING: ANNIS SPRAKELING: KATHEREN
SPRAKELING: MARGERY SPRAKELING FRANCES SPRAKELING
MARGARET SPRAKELING: HANNA SPRAKELING. WHO
DIED ONE THE 7TH DAY OF APRILL AGED 58.
Salutis nostre 1610

IMAGE - SPRACKLING FAMILY PLAQUE IN ST LAURENCE-IN-THANET CHURCH, RAMSGATE © BRIAN WHITEHEAD

I shall ask one of the staff to serve a bottle of our finest wine at this evening's meal and the following entertainment…

… My husband seems particularly fractious this evening, having devoured not only the wine I had brought up from the cellar but another three bottles whilst not partaking of much food. He has argued with his friend, who drank even more, and has now dismissed most of the staff for the evening. This does not bode well for the mummers should they not please him.

As I stand looking over our estate, I notice that no-one is to be seen – the parkland is empty. As I wonder at this, a small noise behind me catches my attention. My husband is requiring my presence in the kitchen.

Whilst sitting listening to my husband's ravings about one of our staff I grow fatigued and attempt to leave and that is when he begins hitting me with cook's meat cleaver. It is most violent and unexpected and my arm is severed but instead of helping me, he is hitting me even more.

He continues to hack at me with the cleaver, wiping my blood onto the comatose figure of his inebriated friend.

I am watching my own death.

He turns his attention to the dogs…

… it is such a wonderful day today and the weather is exceedingly clement.

I

am the Ramsgate Obelisk standing sentinel over the Harbour and beyond. My raison d'être was King George IV's visit in 1821 when he *graciously condescended* to cross the English Channel from Ramsgate en route for Hanover.

(Some say he was trying to avoid his Queen, but that's another story.)

Nowadays I watch over the yachts and motorboats

The Ramsgate Obelisk

In the smart
marina, but I
remember when
the little ships
sailed to rescue
our stranded
soldiers.

Behind me there
is nothing but
sadness.
Gone is the fun
casino, the candy
floss, toffee apples
and Kiss me Kwik.
Gone is Merrie
England, now a
deserted,
unfinished
building site.
And the Great Wall
of Ramsgate
desecrated, the
people's pictures
wantonly
destroyed.

If I were to speak
out, there are tales
I could tell.
But here I stand mute.
Always watchful.

Rosemary Clarke-Jones

20 August 1939 to 19 March 2020

Rosemary was a regular contributor to
IsleWrite and her pieces appeared in
several anthologies and the IsleWrite
exhibition at The Custom House where *The
Ramsgate Obelisk* lent itself perfectly to be
reproduced for sale as a bookmark.

The One in Forty Thousand

Niki Sakka

Niki is a Cypriot who lives in England. Her life's journey has led her through interesting, happy times but also challenging situations, like living in a war-zone and becoming a refugee. Those experiences became the inspiration for her writing. Her stories have been published in several group anthologies.

Niki believes writing is a joyful expression of thoughts and can be cathartic during difficult times.

> **IF A TURKISH SOLDIER FINDS ANYONE WANDERING OUTSIDE THE INHABITED AREA OF THE VILLAGE HE HAS THE *OBLIGATION* TO SHOOT THAT PERSON DEAD IMMEDIATELY.**

It was April 1975. No-one was allowed to go out into the countryside or to the seaside. The military rule from the invaders was loud and clear. The Turkish troops were still camping at the barracks in Akrades. This region of Karpassia, like the whole north part of Cyprus, was occupied by the Turks. Meetings organised by the United Nations searching for common ground and the establishment of peace between Greek Cypriot and Turkish leaders were proving fruitless. People prayed at home and in every church for a fair solution, for an ending to that chaotic political situation created by the Turkish invasion. And above all, prayers were sent to God for the safe return of all the prisoners and missing people.

I was still waiting for permission from the Turkish Military authorities to leave the North and, of course, permission from the Greek Cypriot government to allow me to move to the southern part of Cyprus. That was the procedure regarding Cypriot movements since the island had been divided by the Green Line. Free movement of the islanders around their own homeland was forbidden; another impractical and heartbreaking outcome of the invasion.

My father, with permission from the Turkish local authorities, was getting ready for silk production. He had to assemble the traditional Dulappi. There were different ways for silk production but my father, like his father and sister, used the Dulappi. He had set it up under the shade of a big apricot tree in the back yard of our house.

First, he built a base where he could light the open fire. On top of that, he secured the *leni* (the metal basin), where the silk cocoons would be boiled. Their silk fibres would soften and unwind easily to produce continuous strands or filaments without break. Then my Dad added the wooden frame with the reels. Next to that, he attached the big spinning wheel. The silk thread would hold up there until the end of the whole process. His helper - the second important person in this process - would turn it continually, using a metal handle.

The day before the silk farmer came with his cocoons, my Dad gathered together all the necessary tools. He piled up logs close by for the fire. During the production he needed to add more wood to keep the fire burning continually. He had ready two slippery skinless sticks from *pikrodaphni* (rose-bay). With those, Dad caught the fibres and twisted them before feeding them to the reels for spinning into a single thread. That part was crucial and required special techniques to manage it correctly.

He got three buckets ready. One was for the extra cocoons. He had them close to him so he could add more to the basin when they were needed. The second bucket was for the cold water and the one with the lid on was for the *boumbouries*, the pupae.

He also had ready two gourds with long handles. One gourd looked like a cup. He used it to add cold water or throw out hot water from the basin, to maintain a steady temperature. The other gourd had holes, like a colander. He used that to collect the pupae from the basin and put them into the bucket with a lid.

The right temperatures and the cleanliness of the basin's water, free of pupae, was important for producing good quality silk thread.

The pupae had a strong, horrible smell, like rotten meat or smelly seaweed, but they were the best meze, a delicacy for fish. Usually, my Dad and other family friends and neighbours used them as bait for fishing.

One morning, Dad announced that Maria from Rizokarpasso was going to come to Agios Andronikos that day. She was a silk farmer and one of my father's best clients.

'How? There aren't any buses,' was my Mum's first reaction.

'So? She has a tractor ...'

'A tractor!? She is coming on a tractor? On her own? Escorted by an armed soldier?'

'Yes. She'll be escorted by a soldier. But it's going to be all right. He will be on his own, in a whole group of Greeks. Probably be more

. . >

scared than us. There is no reason for us to panic,' Dad said with emphasis. Then he added, 'Anyway, if it's safe enough for Maria to travel more than twenty-five miles alone with him, I'm sure it would be safe enough for us too.'

'I can't believe that. I admire that she is brave enough to sleep even in a cemetery alone if it's needed, but to drive a tractor by herself with an armed enemy by her side, in a war zone, is something beyond my imagination...' Mum made the sign of the cross three times across her chest.

Soon after that, Maria arrived with her escort and a lot of cocoons. The soldier was young, probably a bit older than me, in his mid-twenties. Handsome with a gentle personality, he was armed but wasn't scary at all.

When Dad and Maria were getting ready for the silk production the soldier introduced himself. He was a Turkish Cypriot from a nearby village. Like all Turkish Cypriots he was able to communicate fluently in the Greek Cypriot dialect whereas we knew no Turkish at all.

As soon as my mother heard his name her facial expression changed. She seemed overwhelmed but it was difficult for me to know why.

She started to tell him about a Turkish Cypriot childhood friend who had a father with the same name as his. Then, she started to describe the beautiful times they had together. Their houses had shared the same yard so from the moment they woke up till bedtime they were inseparable. When the adults were working out in the fields, she and her friend had done everything side by side, cleaning, cooking,

baking cakes, doing embroidery and crochet. They visited friends, shared quality time and made unforgettable memories. Then a few years later, the Turkish family moved to another village, the one that the soldier came from.

Mum was born in 1912 and her friend was a similar age. Communication in the twenties in Cyprus wasn't easy at all, so Mum had lost touch with her dearest friend but she had never forgotten her.

I'd never heard about that childhood friend before. I'd never heard of the two houses with the same yard, although I grew up and lived in that neighbourhood for twelve years until we moved to Agios Andronikos, my father's place.

Mum was a scaredy cat but she was fine in a secure environment, under my Dad's protection and surrounded by people she knew and trusted. Probably the fact of having that stranger, an armed soldier from the opposite side, right on her doorstep, was too much for her. I honestly thought that Mum had lost it and had created that story to disarm the Turk.

I wished I could find a way to convince her that we were safe and there was no reason to be scared, no reason for tales and myths.

The soldier didn't accept anything to eat and would only drink water from the tap in the garden. My Dad said he was welcome to have any fruit he liked from the trees but he wouldn't. He listened quietly to my mother's stories. I wondered if he thought that Mum was a nut case.

Maria had too many cocoons so she would need to come back a few more times.

. . >

FROM SUNSET UNTIL SUNRISE PEOPLE ARE NOT ALLOWED TO OPEN THEIR OUTSIDE DOOR. THE OUTSIDE DOOR SHOULD NOT BE OPENED EVEN IF SOMEONE KNOCKS ON IT. TURKISH SOLDIERS WILL SHOOT DEAD ANYONE WHO OPENS THEIR OUTSIDE DOOR.

The curfew made people's life a misery because the yard was part of the main living area. The water, the loo and other important things were kept outside. It was far harder for old or disabled people, or for those with young children or animals who needed looking after. Some family homes had three rooms but every room had only an outside door. The family was trapped for long hours in one room.

That afternoon, my Dad had to stop early enough so Maria had time to return to her home and get ready before sunset to close her outside door until the next sunrise. So silk production was only possible for a few hours each day.

The next day, Maria came back. She was escorted by the same soldier. I was worried what my mother would do.

The soldier jumped off the tractor, a broad smile on his face. He approached my mum. 'You know something? Your childhood friend *is* my mother.'

'WHAT?'

'That was my reaction too when mum told me. I was dead surprised. I told her what you said yesterday,' he said to my mum.

'Oh God!' Eyes full of joy, she opened her arms and hugged him. 'My dear friend's son...'

'Believe me, I've never seen my mother so happy, ever. She was so excited and couldn't stop crying. She remembered every detail of those years you spent together. They were the best ones in her whole life. She sends her love.'

I was speechless filled with waves of guilt for doubting my mother's sanity.

There were forty-thousand Turkish troops in Cyprus. What were the chances that out of all of them, the one who escorted Maria to our home would be the son of my mother's childhood friend from five decades ago?

I found it unbelievable. But it was true - pure serendipity.

When I asked about their houses my mum said that they had been demolished before I was born which explained why I didn't know about them. With her explanation about some of the details and the confirmation from mum's friend, everything made sense.

Every time Maria came, the same soldier escorted her. After that discovery of our mothers' connection, he felt completely relaxed, accepting food and drink. My parents treated him like their own nephew. My mother and he spent hours and hours chatting about old times. He opened his heart to her.

Even now thinking about the coincidence I struggle to believe it.

The experience led to my belief that politics, religion and custom sometimes become a barrier separating people, poisoning human feelings and turning us against one another.

Lydia Dunn

Lydia has been a member of IsleWrite from the beginning. Always an avid reader, she started writing once the family of six boys she and Charlie had were grown up. Lydia now has thirty-seven grand and great-grandchildren. Her account of a Greenwich childhood, evacuation to Sissinghurst then leaving school at fourteen to work in the Soho rag trade depicts the significant changes that have taken place over the last ninety years.

Lydia's paintings inspired an IsleWrite publication *Dancing with Lydia* and her snapshots of life have featured in many anthologies.

By the Light

The pie-man on his nightly round rings his bell and draws the penniless kids to the warmth of his take-away, an oven carried on the front of his tricycle. Hands warm but stomachs empty they return to their games until one by one, as the night draws in, their parents call them indoors.

A rope suspended from the arm of the lamp-post, hangs abandoned by the would-be Tarzans who had swung mimicking the apeman's call. Giggling girls had huddled aside, pretending not to notice the display intended to impress them.

Echoes of doors being latched, bolts drawn and curtains closed. Just chinks of light from the row of terraced houses leaving only the moths and shadows to play in the lamplight.

The street lamp sheds a circle on the pavement making the stones appear white, set in the darkness around. The quietness is broken only by the nocturnal calls of cats on the prowl.

Patricia Mahoney

Patricia was born in Ottawa, Canada and moved to London, England to pursue a career in the performing arts. She has worked in both countries as a senior arts manager, artistic director, actor, director and playwright. Five of her plays have been professionally produced in her native Canada. Patricia is also an award - winning writer of short stories, poetry and flash fiction - many of which have been published in the UK and Canada.

Most Recent:
2020 - Shortlisted for The Billy Roche International Short Play Award.
2019 - Winner - Dee May Award for Fiction.

Full of Grace is the title story from Patricia's collection of short stories set in the 1950s and 60s, about a young Canadian girl, Mary Margaret, and her journey from inquisitive child to young woman - with a stopover in gawky adolescence. The book comes with an accompanying CD of Patricia reading these reflective stories. You can listen to a couple by visiting *patriciamahoney.com*.

Full of Grace

'Mary Margaret, if you don't know the words to a song, please do not attempt to sing.'

It was summer and eight year old Mary Margaret was in a good mood. Her parents had just left and she was helping her Great Aunt Greta with the washing up. It was her first time away from home and she'd been looking forward to enjoying two weeks away. She hadn't noticed that she'd been singing. She stopped and they finished the washing up in silence.

'Well, let's get you settled in then.'

Mary Margaret collected her suitcase and struggled with it up the main staircase behind her Aunt Greta. She'd discovered a back staircase off the kitchen but had been instructed that she was 'not to use it under any circumstances'.

As her Great Aunt Grace was away at the cottage for the summer, it had been agreed that Mary Margaret would have her bedroom. Aunt Greta opened the door. Mary Margaret stood in the doorway and gawped. It was so beautiful - like something out of a magazine. The walls were a deep Wedgwood blue trimmed in white. The furniture: an enormous bed, a dresser and a vanity table with a little bench in front were also white. There was nothing on any of the glass-covered surfaces except a white porcelain figure of a young woman wearing a long flowing dress and holding on to her bonnet. She was lovely - a proper lady - everything that Mary Margaret now realised Aunt Greta expected her to be - well mannered, 'full of grace' and silent.

IMAGE - COVER DESIGN © ANDY BESWICK PHOTO © KEITH RENNIE

Jill Anabona Smith

Jill started writing on a University of Kent at Canterbury Combined Studies Creative Writing course. Since then, she has won numerous prizes in fiction competitions run by BBC Radio Nottingham, story-tellers. co.uk, Ramsgate Royal Harbour Heritage Festival, the Winchester Annual Writers' Conference, Kent Life and Writing magazine. Novelist Louise Doughty *Apple Tree Yard* said in the Sunday Telegraph that Jill's writing 'made her flesh creep'. Jill took this as a compliment.

Jill became involved in co-ordinating IsleWrite from its inception.

A Gentleman's Car

When I was twelve, I had to say we lived on the corner of Park Road.

Actually, our front door was in the High Street but Mother said it sounded nicer.

As she watched the toast didn't burn under the grill, she glanced out of the window. 'Oh, I *say*.'

'Eh?'

'Elbows *off* the table, Susan. And it's 'pardon', not 'eh'.

'Someone's moving into the house opposite. With a nice little girl. They look very suitable,' she approved.

A *'nice' little girl*. Boring, more like.

Next morning, a lanky, black-haired girl, wearing a crisper version of my uniform, came out of the house in Park Road.

We spoke together. ''Lo.'

'You too?' she gestured to her blazer pocket badge.

With a world-weary nod intended to convey that, after nearly two years, I knew everything there was to know about the Girls' Grammar, I looked her over. Skinny wrists protruded from the unyielding newness of green serge. 'How old are you?'

'Nearly thirteen,' she offered, adding as

we looked right, left, then right again, 'Maureen Browne-with-an-e.'

'I'm Susan. Anyway,' I pointed, 'you can't wear *that*.'

On her third, grimy-nailed finger, the ring's bright green stone twinkled in the May sunshine.

She rolled her eyes. 'My Dad. We move a lot – for his work. So he buys me things. They won't let me wear that, Dad, I said. He said *You wear it. They're just jealous, teachers.*'

With growing respect for my new friend, I decided not to tell Mother about that.

'Browne with an e?' she mused that night.

'I wish I could afford his car,' Daddy observed from behind the Daily Mail. 'It's the latest model. The P6 2000. Quite the thing.'

Mother's eyes flashed. '*Is* it?'

He looked up startled. 'Well, it's a *Rover*, dear. A gentleman's car.'

Whether it was the car or the e, I never knew, but Maureen's visa was stamped Approved. 'Why not ask her round to tea?' Mother smiled brightly.

But I went to her house first.

'Oh dear... the potatoes...' Mrs. Browne, a wraithlike, transparent woman slid absent-mindedly out of the room.

Slabs of liver rested, grey and limp on my chilly plate. 'I don't eat liver,' I whispered.

Under that dark fringe, Maureen's eyes darted to the door. 'You've got to. Mum's a bit funny... she'll have one of her turns...'

'Can't.'

Tight-lipped, she reached over with her fork. 'Give it here.'

I was chasing the last of the peas round my plate when Mrs. Browne came back, a limp hand to her temple. 'Now... what...?'

Maureen burped, 'Potatoes, Mum. But me and Susan have finished, haven't we?'

As I nodded, the dining room door swung open.

'Uh-oh,' Maureen muttered.

'Maureen, my darling,' the man in the pinstriped suit boomed, then the dazzling smile beneath his coal-black moustache flashed at me. 'And this must be Susan,' he gripped my hand and I caught a whiff of something like Christmas pudding.

Glancing at our grey-green smeared plates, he told his wife hurriedly, 'No – not for me. Lunch with a customer today. Still full.'

'They say I can go. In the car, next Sunday.' A few weeks later, I was desperate to join the trip celebrating the end of term. 'They're having a picnic...'

'Well...' Mother wavered.

'*Please?*'

'See what your father says.'

And, of course, because it was a Rover, he said yes.

It smelt of men, somehow. Of hide and oil and ashtrays and spanners. The wipers' hypnotic sweep swished at the warm rain and, cocooned by steamed-up windows and thick wool carpet, Maureen and I rolled from side to side on the conker-shiny back seat as the Rover burbled between Kentish hedgerows.

'It was nice when we left,' Mrs. Browne

. . >

reminisced wistfully.

'Stop complaining,' her husband snapped.

I studied the shiny jet-black of his Brylcreemed head, mesmerised by the narrow band of pale roots shimmering along the razor-sharp parting.

He took a slim, silvery case from his pocket and flipped it open, like in a film. 'Light me one.'

'Er...' His wife looked around nervously.

He jabbed at a black bakelite knob on the dashboard. 'There.'

With trembling fingers she placed the lit cigarette between his lips and as smoke wreathed around the car, they sat in silence, ignoring us.

'Your legs are really thin,' I looked enviously at the pearly skin on display beneath Maureen's shorts. My own thighs spread, pink and pudgy, beside them.

'S'pose,' she shrugged.

'Did you watch Dr Kildare? On Thursday night?' I whispered behind my hand. 'When he kissed that patient? They were really in love. Dr. Gillespie came in just as he was going to lose control and go all the way,' I babbled.

'It's just telly, Susan,' Maureen said sharply.

Crestfallen, I glanced up to see Mr. Browne's eyes in the rear-view mirror, laughing at his daughter and her silly friend.

At Alkham, the sun broke through the clouds and we bounced over the ruts at the entrance to a field. The air was fresh and clear after the car and we chose the farthest corner, down by the river, for our picnic.

With a flourish, Maureen's father shook out the travel rug. 'Girls - your magic carpet awaits.'

'My Dad says your car's the bee's knees, Mr. Browne,' I smiled up at him.

'Ah, there's a man who knows his onions,' he nodded. 'Matter of fact, I'm in the trade. If your father's looking for a new motor car, I'd be happy to take him for a spin in her. Just send him along to the A&B Garage.'

'Oh,' I blurted, 'he can't afford to buy one.'

'Ah,' he slid an arm round my shoulder and squeezed, 'have to rely on Ernie coughing up, eh? Right well, I'll get the basket — '

' — oh, let me help,' I rushed, desperate to compensate for my father's penury.

There was one of those tiny pauses you only remember when you think about it all afterwards.

'Good girl, Susan. Maureen — ' he barked, 'keep an eye on her.' He nodded to the riverbank where Mrs. Browne, reed-like herself, gazed down into the dappled water.

I ran to catch up as he marched back to the car. The shiny, dark green bootlid swung up and I stretched in eagerly, puffing slightly.

'Better check...' he said knowingly, and Old Spice swirled around me as his long arm outreached mine to lift the wicker lid. There was only a jar of meat paste and a green plastic flask, tea seeping steadily from the greaseproof paper around its cork.

He seemed unsurprised. 'Looks like ices on the pier again.'

Oh,' I gushed, 'ices would be lovely.'

That moustache glistened as he said appreciatively, 'You're quite the young lady, Susan. You know that though, eh?' he growled. 'Popular with the boys, I bet. I saw you looking at me...' Gripping my wrist, he swung me round to face him, pushing me backwards and

. . >

I gasped as the cool metal of the Rover's wing pressed against the backs of my legs. 'Like to try a real man now?'

'I…'

There was a thin cry, from somewhere a long way away.

' — Come on, now. I heard your little chat,' he said thickly. 'All the way, eh?' Somehow, his feet had got between mine, his trousers scratchy between my knees.

'Dad!' Maureen's voice was closer now. 'Mum's fallen in!'…

Naturally, I'd been warned, in embarrassed undertones, about men. And read the letters in the back of Jackie about what happened when men lost respect for a girl.

If only that silly woman hadn't lost her balance…

Surely thinking the same thing, he drove in fast, furious silence, obviously too preoccupied to catch my eyes in the mirror. Pale, play-acting Dr. Kildare was left behind - Maureen had been right, that was just telly.

My heart was so loud I thought everyone could hear it.

This was The Real Thing.

'Shall I come round to play next week?' I asked eagerly, as her mother trailed miserably indoors.

Maureen shook her head sadly. 'I'll be busy.'

'My, *what* an adventure.' Mother put beans on toast in front of me.

I stared down at the brown lino, replaying the delicious scene over in my mind. Oh, there'd be difficulties, but he'd wait for me to turn sixteen, I just knew, then people would see we were meant to be together.

'Early night for you, young lady,' Mother cleared the untouched supper away. 'Too much excitement for one day.'

'Aren't you going to play with Maureen?' she quizzed me on the Monday morning.

'She's busy,' I mumbled miserably.

By the evening though, I'd thought up an excuse - a homework project, I said.

Heart thumping, I willed him to open the door.

But Maureen answered my persistent ring.

She wouldn't be coming out to play, she glanced over her shoulder. Her mother'd be ill for some time. Maureen would have to be the lady of the house, her Dad had said.

Before long, the summer had slipped away and then the day before the Autumn Term began, there was a removal van outside their house.

At lunchtime, Mother poured custard over my apple pie then, still nursing the jug, wandered absent-mindedly over to the window and stood watching Mr. Browne, dashing even in his shirtsleeves, directing operations. 'I can understand them promoting him,' she sighed wistfully. 'A manager's post in Eastbourne, they said in the corner shop.

She was rather unfortunate… but he was a real gentleman.'

Denise Gow

Denise loves writing for pleasure, sometimes for pay and occasionally for awards. She's tempted by short stories, novels, plays, TV and screenplays.

She served her apprenticeship at *The Creative Business* going on to write episodes of *Emmerdale*. Her screenplays have been commissioned and optioned. Denise has also directed many commercials for household products from *Fairy Liquid* to *Baby Bio* and multi award-winning *Equilon* a product for Irritable Bowel Syndrome while managing to avoid the condition herself.

Denise's novel: *The Lost Madonna* can be found at *denisegow.co.uk* .

The Hue of Yellow

Shards of sunlight pierced through the wooden shutters of Mark's attic studio reflecting on the gold of scattered Renaissance and icon style paintings.

Being a converted chapel it was cold so Mark lit a potbellied stove adding dried rosemary to the embers making the room smell of aromatic wood smoke which mingled with the prickly scent of turpentine. He tidied the jars of vibrant coloured pigment which lined his shelves before seating himself at his paint splattered work table.

Once settled he picked up a fresh egg from a wicker basket and held it in his hand to warm it before cracking it open. Discarding the egg white into an empty blue and white china bowl, he rolled the moist yolk from palm to palm letting it leave its sticky outer membrane in his hands. It gave a soft reassuring feel. He was always amazed at how well the liquid stayed within its sac. Like a worshipper fingering a favourite rosary, he rolled it across his palms some more for pleasure. Pinching a corner of the yolk between his forefinger and thumb, he lifted it out of his palm. The sac drooped like a fat teardrop. He pierced the bottom end with his fingernail, which enabled the oily golden fluid to flow into a clean bowl underneath. *Plop.*

He needed a clear mind to paint an icon and

this was the traditional way he slowed his thoughts and prepared himself to contact his muse. Opening a new packet of pigment, he scooped a few ounces of cadmium onto a blade and bridled at the acid yellow hue. Staring at it uncomfortably, his composure lost, he remembered…

… the day of the outing with the yellow tablecloth when teenagers were kissing on the grass nearby and his mother was becoming agitated. His father sat dead still, holding onto his braces, remaining as patient as he could be, waiting for his food, waiting for everything to be deemed perfect. He'd driven such a long way and on the new motorway too, to be beside the river on the grass, for a picnic. But on his special day off, his head began to hang low like it did when he was sad and hiding it.

'The sun is getting in my eyes,' Mother said. So they turned the gingham tablecloth this way and that and shuffled round themselves so the sun wouldn't hurt her eyes. Mark then had to strain to see what the teenage boy with his girlfriend was doing with his tongue. Father was salivating over a sausage roll, but he waited until everything was set just right so that mother would be pleased.

'Behaving like dogs,' mother said as she patted and straightened the tablecloth all over again. But Mark couldn't see any dogs and was taking a dislike to the yellow in the wax cloth he was staring at, and now his tummy was rumbling as well.

'It doesn't have to spoil our day,' Father said. He opened his napkin then folded it up again to try and forget his hunger.

'Oh, look there's a boat,' she said, trying to use anything that went by to distract from the couple lying on the grass. Mark became fascinated by the length of the boy's tongue and didn't understand why he put it in the girl's ear, and why she didn't mind.

'Where's Lisa?' his mother suddenly cried out.

Mark looked round but couldn't see his sister.

She'd disappeared again. She hated rows and never really liked to eat out in the open.

'She always disappears when food is ready.' Mother's voice was high pitched, kind of strangulated.

'I'll go look for her,' Mark said, knowing it was an offer his mother couldn't object to.

He got up and started vaguely looking. Once out of sight he slipped off his socks and then let the grass tickle his toes through his sandals. He wandered enjoying the freedom - glad to get away from the tension of the picnic and his mother's white gloves and her smoothing out the cloth and dusting off invisible insects.

Passing other families laughing, he noticed some children had jam on their faces but it didn't seem to matter - their mother wasn't angry. They could still sit there and eat and talk and play. He took time looking at the families who were enjoying the sunny day. He paused and watched the sky, the high drifting clouds and listened secretly to the squeals of children playing around him. There was no need to find his sister straight away as then he'd have to go back and sit quietly beside the tablecloth and eat cold food and endure the fuss and his sister would be unhappy too.

People started shouting, not the children, but the sound of adults and dogs all jumbled together. A man was running to the riverside. A woman whose arms had got caught up in her pinafore was trying to point to the water and screaming. Others came to join her. There was a lot of noise and confusion. Mark walked toward them in his dreamy, summer's day mood.

'A girl,' he heard them say. He thought someone might be swimming, but he knew it couldn't be Lisa as she couldn't swim.

Surprisingly, a man took off his jacket and trousers and jumped into the water swimming so strongly about ten feet out. His Labrador barked at the river's bank. The man dived under the water and it seemed he wasn't going to come up - just his hat, which he'd forgotten to take off, floated around lost on the surface, driving his dog wild. Eventually, the dog jumped in too and swam toward the hat. Everyone moved closer to the river's edge, suddenly quiet. Then the man surfaced with a body in his arms. A girl. Mark could see her hair and it reminded him of Lisa but didn't think it was possible that it could be her, yet it looked like her. And everyone started to look round, in

his direction. He froze, found he couldn't move. It was as if his feet were nailed to the ground, and he had to stand there witnessing the events that were happening: the man bringing the girl out of the water, water pouring from them, the women crying, the wet dog with a hat in its jaw. The next thing he remembered - he was hit on the head and then seemed to sway a little bit. His mother and father went by. His mother had hit him. His father was well out of breath with sweat beads at his temples. He watched as his mum and dad ran up to the people with the girl's body and started crying. Mother even let her white cotton gloves get wet as she stroked the girl's hair. Kneeling on the ground with the girl they leaned over and touched her and Mark watched how affectionate they were with her. And he wanted to be there with them too but was so puzzled why he couldn't move. He tried to lift his feet but they wouldn't budge and his jaw became fixed in his face. Everything was moving in slow motion, if only he could get things to run backwards.

A screaming ambulance arrived and several men opened the back. After a while, one of the men in uniform came over and stood beside Mark. He was glad he hadn't been hit again.

'Your sister has drowned,' the officer said leaning down to him, placing a hand on his shoulder which helped him to loosen and move. Mark nodded, still unable to speak. They walked calmly to the ambulance together. Once inside, his mother stared, his father stared too, but they didn't speak. The way they looked at Mark, it seemed they thought it was all his fault. Perhaps it was. He sat down on the hard bench seat in the ambulance and allowed himself to realise the dreadful truth: if he'd got there sooner perhaps he might've been able to save her. But he had just been wandering, enjoying the summer's day and couldn't have known she was going swimming and was getting into trouble. He hid his face and looked down at his lap, picked away at the threads of his socks until his father stopped him.

Back home, in his bedroom he ran over everything again in his head. He would've done everything for his sister if he'd known and would've drowned instead of her if he could. He shook with the memories and started feeling ice cold. After getting warm in his bed he hid his head underneath the pillow and felt something there, some paper. It was a note folded over. It seemed to be in his sister's handwriting. He switched on the side light, unfurled it and read:

I can't take anymore. The bullies have won and Mum and Dad won't listen. I can't tell them about the things that are happening and I feel I am letting them down so this is best. I love two things - Tugs and you, my dear soppy brother. I can't carry on. I want to join the Angels.

Love Lisa.

He never read the note to them, perhaps it was best they thought about her the way they did. He assumed the guilt for his sister's death and over time he almost believed it. They buried the memory of her that day and she was hardly mentioned again as the grief and the sadness was too much to bear.

… Mark looked at the paint he had mixed, the colour was softer now, and the yellow had lost its acid hue. He'd often wondered why he could have such a negative reaction to some yellows. He flipped open a leather folder containing sheets of gold leaf and pulled out the old, faded letter from all those years ago. A calm ethereal voice spoke to him.

It wasn't your fault. Stop blaming yourself. I'm always with you — think of me as being just next door.

Peace like an ocean wave washed over him and he crumpled the letter - let it go. Then, with a clear mind, he loaded his paintbrush with glistening tempera and blessed his sister as he applied a confident stroke to his board - a nearly finished portrait of Lisa, painted with a golden aura. Grateful to be absorbed in his work, he continued.

THE HUE OF YELLOW WON THE FOLKESTONE LITERARY FESTIVAL SHORT STORY COMPETITION. IT WAS ADAPTED FROM A PASSAGE IN DENISE'S NOVEL *THE LOST MADONNA*. AMAZON.CO.UK - *THE LOST MADONNA*. KINDLE ASIN: B078HGX4VG
INFORMATION ABOUT *THE LOST MADONNA*, HER OTHER WRITING AND HER RECENT PLAY *THE MUSIC OF MATHEMATICS* ABOUT THE LIFE AND WORK OF ADA LOVELACE AND HER FRIENDSHIP WITH CHARLES DICKENS CAN BE FOUND AT DENISEGOW.CO.UK

Heather Hunt

Heather and her twin were born in *Kabwe* (formerly Broken Hill), *Zambia* (Northern Rhodesia) in 1939. She married a local farmer, also Kabwe-born and became very involved in agricultural politics. For twenty-five years she represented farmers on boards made up of government officials and crop farmers acting on behalf of the industry. She enjoyed the challenge of directorship, despite being the only female and often the only white representative.

After her husband passed away she moved to Margate in 2014.

Heather has always written and her stories are inspired by her life in Africa.

The Secret Dance

'Let's go for a walk.'

It was one of those rare times when Des and I could relax without the demands of the farm taking priority. The dogs raced around, excited that the master was joining us for our daily walk. We crossed the road, took the path to the base of the kopjie, a rocky outcrop, part of the Rift Valley which erupted in ancient times dividing the African continent.

Our farm had three sections of these rocky hills, not very high, running from East to West, dividing the farm, with fields in between.

It was about 4pm as we climbed the gentle slope. The rains were over. The air was cool with just a hint of winter around the corner, the trees still green, the grass had not dried and late summer flowers still bloomed. Once at the top, we looked down.

It was fairly flat and we could walk almost to the farm boundary, above the surrounding area, no one would know we were there. It was lovely, a breeze ruffled the leaves with a whisper. A golden oriole warbled his liquid song and a boubou shrike called his mate. She replied immediately and they flew off.

We walked in silence, ahead of us the dogs were barking at the hyraxes and were scolded in turn from a branch, safely out of reach. They disturbed a nightjar crouched amongst the rocks and it flew up with a clatter of wings. I happened to look down to a small clearing.

The farm flock of sheep were grazing and Lazarus, the shepherd, was dancing to music only he could hear.

Lazarus appeared at the farm looking for work about five years previously. The Kapitou (the name given to the man in charge of the labour) suggested he would be ideal as the shepherd. He was good at that job, his only failing, a fondness for the local brew. However, he never failed to take the flock out.

His black coat, far too big for his slight body, flew around him as he twirled about. His shoes flapped but did not fall off. One of the sheep lifted its head, looked at the prancing man and then resumed grazing. Lazarus continued, it was a moving sight, this little man dancing gracefully with only the trees and sheep as an audience. We stood for a while and then continued our walk. The dogs had bounded ahead.

We reached the boundary and turned to walk home. The sun was setting and fingers of glorious colour stretched across the sky. A flock of egrets flew to their evening roost on the farm lake. We called the dogs and they scampered up, tongues hanging out, tired from their run.

We ambled back and watched Lazarus put the sheep into their enclosure in the farmyard.

Dishonest Indian: Grey Owl, my mother and me

This flimsy 14-page souvenir booklet was published in 1937 to mark the occasion of Grey Owl's second tour of the United Kingdom.

Its discovery was the result of a long, hard search on my part; snatched from the hands of another, equally anxious bidder on eBay at the last second or two. Doubtless I paid well over the odds for it, but with reasonable justification. Subsequent searches with no result attest to its rarity despite the fact that they were probably printed in their hundreds, if not thousands. Grey Owl's published books, however, are still relatively easy to obtain, and with several subsequent biographies on the market, it is clear that interest in this charismatic early pioneer of nature conservation and education remains strong.

The reason why I wanted it so badly was because as a child, I grew up with another copy that belonged to my mother. It was kept in the bottom drawer of my parents' heavy dark-wood sideboard, along with her button box and a souvenir brochure for the 1951 Festival of Britain. The booklet became something of a talisman for me and I grew up with a keen interest in anything and everything to do with Red

Graham Ward

Graham worked as a freelance illustrator before reverting to his first discipline of painting. He was represented by the Portal Gallery, a long-established British institution specialising in figurative art. His work is held in a number of private collections in the United Kingdom, Europe and the United States. His invented landscapes, often populated by child-kings and Holy fools reflect his abiding fascination with the act of pilgrimage, and in particular, with specific routes to Santiago de Compostela in Northern Spain; journeys throughout Spain and Portugal to the shrine of St James which he has been making on foot since 2004. A long-standing book project on the subject of pilgrimage, *Camino Details* is due for completion in 2020.

Indians (the term 'Native American' not being a concept we fully understood then).

The black and white Westerns of my 50s childhood never seemed to give those poor Indians anything remotely like an even break, and no one but no one seemed to speak up for them. I naturally gravitated toward their teepees, their eagle feathers and their buckskins. Images from the National Geographic, that staple of the dentist's waiting room of the day, also fuelled my passion, somehow painting a far more reasoned existence for the people of the Plains than any John Ford movie could. It would be fair to say until the Beatles were invented, my pin-ups consisted largely of those wondrous Edward Curtis photographs, or else the beautifully rendered watercolour images of 'Indian' encampments by George Caitlin, and my companions those Indian brave and squaw dolls that were a staple of the Woolworth's toy departments of my childhood. I lost count of how many I had; sufficient certainly for a tribe. Their eyes closed when you laid them to sleep, and the squaw had a tiny papoose strapped to her chamois-covered back. Of course, they were all identical, but this was a detail I overcame by adding embellishments to their headgear from the family budgie and providing them with a teepee made from old dusters with sweet-pea stakes for tent poles. An over-zealous Golden Retriever puppy saw many of them off to the Great Beyond (they were, as I recall, relatively fragile; manufactured in Japan or China from that brittle kind of plastic) but as long as Woolworths continued to sell them, I would badger my poor aunt and mother for substitutes.

The booklet I grew up with was probably issued in 1935, two years before the one I now hold in my hand. Not recognising then that the likeness of Grey Owl that comprises the front image was painted by Sir John Lavery, the well-regarded portrait painter of the Edwardian era, I loved it simply for the powerful presence of its sitter,

. . >

gazing out towards the viewer with heavily fringed buckskin sleeves folded across his chest and eagle feathers in his coal-black hair. When I opened the envelope that contained the eBay trophy, it brought back a flood of recollection; about the place where I grew up, my obsession with all things Indian, but most of all, a sense of sadness, as it was the one thing amidst the debris and confusion that my father had failed to find for me when my parents' house had to be cleared. Of all the clutter that could cheerfully have been foregone, this, the flimsiest of ephemeral items had vanished forever, and with it, perhaps for good and all, my childhood.

What my mother's copy contained was a black and white photograph of herself, aged I would guess, around fourteen pictured with Grey Owl himself.

Of course, I questioned my mother about the time he visited the school she attended in Tottenham. She could recall the booklet and even the visit itself, but not the existence of the photograph. I can only imagine that it was a bold step on the part of the school authorities to have a photographer present for an event which must have been a rather magical occurrence - given the everyday-nature of a mid-thirties childhood. I think that it was the loss of this photograph that affected me the most.

We now know much more about the life and works of Grey Owl. History has rather rewritten the story of the pioneer Canadian naturalist, whose mission it was to tour the world in order to bring a greater understanding of the animal kingdom and its workings. He was born Archibald Stansfield Belaney, in 1888 - not of Native American parentage, but in Hastings, East Sussex, and into

a family of farmers. His father drank away what fortune there was, and some sources suggest that Belaney's mother was little more than a child herself when she became pregnant with him. Raised by his grandmother and two maiden aunts, he expressed a keen interest in nature and in native cultures from an early age. He attended Hastings Grammar School until he was sixteen, beginning his working life in the local timber-yard, but, according to an early biographer Lovat Dickenson in 'Wilderness Man' (1974), was dismissed for dropping a bomb down his employer's chimney. Belaney emigrated to Canada in 1906 in order, it was said, to study agriculture. After a spell in Toronto, he moved to Temagami, Northern Ontario and adopted a native American identity and the name for which he would become best-known.

Marrying a member of the Anishinaabe tribe, Angele Egwuna, he then worked as a fur-trapper, a wilderness guide and a forest ranger. He fabricated his past, stating that he had been the child of a Scottish father and an Apache mother, and had emigrated from the U.S. in order to join the Ojibwa people. In World War One, Grey Owl joined the 13th Montreal Battalion of the Black Watch. The unit was shipped to France, where he served as a sniper. His associates always regarded him as having come from Native American stock. He was wounded twice in 1916, and the latter incident resulted in the onset of gangrene, whereafter he was shipped to England in order to receive proper treatment for his injuries. Having been moved from one

Infirmary to another whilst doctors attempted to heal him, he was finally shipped home to Canada in 1917 with an honourable discharge from the army and a disability pension. It was during his time in England that he re-met and subsequently married his childhood friend Constance Holmes, but the marriage was not to last. In 1925, he met Gertrude Bernard, a native of the Iroquois tribe, who encouraged him to stop the fur-trapping which on his return to Canada he had resumed and instead publish his writings about wilderness issues and the lives of animals. As a result, he attracted the attention of the Dominion Parks Service, and he began to work for them as a naturalist. In 1928, the Parks Service made him the subject of a documentary film entitled 'Beaver People', which featured Grey Owl and his wife playing with their pets.

In all aspects of his books and subsequent documentary films, he actively promoted the concept of environmentalism and nature conservation. For the two extensive tours of the United Kingdom - which included a return to his native Hastings - he wore the familiar Ojibwa costume to promote his books and lectures. Still alive, his aunts recognised the prodigal, but remained silent about his origins and upbringing until the end of 1937, when they effectively aided and abetted his unmasking to the media. On the latter tour, he met the young princesses Elizabeth and Margaret at Buckingham Palace. Exhausted from his journeys up and down the UK, he returned to Canada, and to his cabin at Ajawaan Lake, and died the following year of pneumonia on April 13th. He is buried in the grounds of his lakeside retreat. After his death, questions began to arise as to his true identity, and a local newspaper 'The North Bay Nugget' ran an exposé. The story was soon taken up by national and then international organisations, including the London 'Times'.

Lovat Dickenson, his publisher, attempted to maintain Grey Owl's chosen identity, but was forced to admit that his friend had lied to him also. 'Grey Owl' was indeed a fabrication; an invented Indian like so many others. Consequences of the revelations were dramatic; an immediate cessation of his book publications, and in some instances, with extant copies being withdrawn from sale. As a result, donations for conservation causes that Grey Owl had been so anxious to promote were very badly affected.

Richard Attenborough (who recalled meeting Grey Owl as a fifteen-year old boy) made a film of his life in 1999. It received mixed reviews and was not shown in the U.S. On the 100th anniversary of his birth, a Canadian Red Maple tree was planted in the grounds of Hastings Grammar School, and in 1997, the mayor of Hastings unveiled a plaque dedicated to Grey Owl on the house in which he was born. In the town's museum is a full-sized replica of his Canadian lakeside dwelling, with a display of memorabilia including a selection of his published works and I believe, a copy of this brochure.

I am very fortunate to have found another copy.

When it first arrived, I carefully turned the pages – it was in excellent condition. Then something dropped out – a ticket for Grey Owl's appearance at Shire Hall in 1937. The ticket date was for December 11th – my mother's birthday.

. . /

Three Kisses

We parked the old Morris Minor at the end of Miller's Dale and walked in the fresh mountain air along the valley. The conifers and crags and rippling streams filled us with joy and blossoming love. We ate fresh apricots from a brown paper bag, because she fancied them.

  As we reached the head of the Dale we paused and looked at the footpath rising to the pass. We held hands and then, taking her duffel-coated body to my threadbare anorak, I kissed her for the first time. Cold lips, blocked noses and the taste of apricots.

Stock still,
Tattooed arms locked,
Tear-soaked faces,
The sun glinting
On their studs and rings,
Lips carefully joined
In a Chinese puzzlement.

The hire van loaded,
The 'To Let' sign planted,
The end of the path.
The end of love.

It's over now.

    She is lying pale and still in her white bed, her lips no longer moving. A moment before, she had opened her eyes; he leant forward and kissed her.

    A kiss that started a lifetime ago, taken into the darkness and never ending.

Joe Eddington

Joe joined IsleWrite when he retired from general practice. Prior to this he wrote some lighthearted articles for medical journal supplements. His writing now comprises semi-autobiographical stories and poems often featuring his hobbies: walking, swimming and dancing. He says that belonging to IsleWrite has helped the development of his writing and the annual anthology has given him the opportunity to see his work in print and 'One day I'll finish my novel!'

Three Kisses was first published in 2012 and exhibited by IsleWrite at the Marine Studios and the Harbour Arm Gallery, Margate as part of the *Kissed Off* exhibition.

Margaret Mamaki

In 1961, Margaret and Eli, a young British-Nigerian couple moved to Kaduna in northern Nigeria, where Eli, a doctor, started a medical clinic in the centre of town. This narrative documents the journey and experiences of the couple in Kaduna, and offers a personal reflection on forty years of recent Nigerian history and events. Later, the couple bought some farmland, planted orchards and set up a restaurant and a pottery. Their farm was called Jacaranda. Through this work, Margaret became intimately involved with the lives of the village children. *The Jacaranda Children* relates that story, told here in several short excerpts.

The Jacaranda Children

In the beginning, we started to plant our land and build the house. It had just been an empty patch of earth, grazed by Fulani cattle next to a few thatched houses. Over the years, the neighbourhood expanded into a dense settlement of low-cost shacks. Mosques gradually sprang up and the road outside became congested with traffic. A petrol station was built on the opposite corner but in spite of the noise and fumes our garden became a retreat, an oasis set in the confused world.

We planted teak trees and palms to shield us from the noise and they towered under the glaring sun, vines twisting around their massive trunks. Profuse Golden Shower blossoms created an orange iridescent waterfall. Ferns, orchids and leafy creepers grew all over these palms, their struggle to dominate, spread and climb towards the sky creating a tiny jungle. Sunbirds hovered, wings vibrating, dipping their long beaks into the orchids. Beyond an iron gate was a shady courtyard where there was a small pond and fountain. You could see bright red goldfish, the type with telescopic eyes. Purple and cream water lilies covered the surface of the water, their waxy flowers were the armchairs for hundreds of tiny frogs. There was always an intoxicating scent of wild jasmine. This was our home.

• • •

In addition to teaching, Margaret created a pottery to make viable work and an income for local people and she and Eli instigated roving clinics where illness and poverty were rife.

One morning in Damisi village a handsome boy was brought by his father a schoolmaster, for immunisation.

I noticed his legs were abnormally bowed; the profile of the curvature was like a hoop, his knees at least two feet apart. He'd never be able to run or play football, but still smiled. Surely this couldn't be rickets? He looked well-nourished, his skin glossy and there was no shortage of sunshine here.

His father seemed unperturbed. 'There's a village called Kafari where nearly all the children have this disease.'

Another man said 'Two other villages, Telele and Pam Madaki's children have this problem, only worse.'

'I'd like them to come to Jacaranda next week. We'll give them some medicine.' Mentally I added a few extra bottles of cod-liver oil to the requisition list.

The next clinic ran smoothly and as the red sun sank into the harmattan dust, we finished work but the farm gates clattered open and a procession of young children appeared, hobbling and staggering like little trolls, their faces set on reaching me. At least thirty limped through the gates, some with sticks, some carried. A few crawled over the stone ground wearing kneepads cut from old tyres.

The chief of Telele introduced his small son. 'He can't run and will never be able to farm when he grows up.'

'How far is your village from here?' I asked.

He waved towards some distant hills. 'We have been walking since early morning.'

Eli and I agreed we would help these children but the question was how to begin?

• • •

Walking back from a meeting one day where the latest drugs were discussed, Margaret noticed a woman walking towards her...

It was probably her irregular steps that first drew my attention and then she seemed to stagger. Just as I passed she squatted and tugged open her wrapper. I heard her moan and a slimy grey bubble like a balloon dropped onto the path.

I stood mesmerised then stooped to peer. The bubble

. . >

moved so I instinctively pulled its membranes apart. Through the clear birth fluids I saw a tiny pink leg, toes fanning wide, kicking and thrusting as if in anger. Next an elbow, followed by a hand with a perfect set of fingernails. I dragged the rest of the membrane away and saw a beautifully formed head with black curls. As I gathered the tiny mite up it started to roar. I placed him in his mother's arms, inwardly smiling over the generous size of his manhood. Another tiny human had just crash-landed to earth to begin the journey of life.

• • •

There was an outbreak of cholera near the villages she loved and concerned that a stream would bring the disease, Margaret determined to bring vaccine to them.

In brilliant sunshine and intense heat I left home with a driver and Nurse Isa. Although short in stature, he carried the heavy cold boxes with ease.

I knew thunderstorms would follow. We parked the vehicle on higher ground as lightning hit the granite hills and the downpour began. Below, the plank bridge was visible only inches above the rushing water. Unloading the syringes and vaccine we walked gingerly down.

We were vulnerable in such an isolated spot and five men in black raincloaks emerged from behind a tree, startling us. I was relieved to find they were young men trained as health workers, who insisted on taking the luggage, insisting on carrying even my small handbag. Two took my hands guiding me over the cascading torrents, my bifocals steamed up and the slippery planks held together with bicycle chains wobbled as we crossed.

Walking through the downpour I heard children's voices singing a beautiful hymn. In the church hundreds of smiling people clapped.

The chief shook our hands and facing the congregation asked me to pray.

At a loss for words, I turned to Nurse Isa. 'You do it. They won't understand my English.' And he rose and prayed as devoutly as any parson.

After the service, the gentle chief organised the waiting line and held each child, soothing some who cried. Women came next, then men. Once all his people had been injected, the Chief took his own vaccination.

On the way home my anxiety changed to relief and I forgot about the mud and slippery path. We savoured the magical experience we had shared together, drunk with happiness. As the planting season ended and the rain subsided I returned to Telele. My beautiful people had not caught cholera.

• • •

But in 2000 the Sharia riots took place and things changed.

As we rounded the bend towards our house, gunfire rang out and the crowds rapidly dispersed into the mosque along the road. We were home.

Jagged holes gaped through the high wall. The smashed gate hung by one dislocated hinge. On it was hooked the wire skeleton of the tyre that had been meant for my husband's neck. In the garden there was a stench of petrol fumes and smoke in a sinister silence. Charred wood, stones, broken glass and rubble littered the ground.

The flame trees and palms still glowed red from the fire. They had faithfully shielded our house from the missiles but with expensive consequence. The creepers and blossoms had been consumed by the flames. I wondered if the tiny tree creatures had escaped. In the courtyard, the pond was half empty, water lilies uprooted. A thick film of petrol floated on the water shrouding hundreds of dead fish. One of our faithful dogs lay dead beside the pond, his fur singed from his body. I had to control my emotions by remembering that humans had also been torched. At that moment a sudden breeze wafted the charred palm fronds and tiny, coiled shreds fell all around us. It was as if the trees were weeping…

THE JACARANDA CHILDREN IS AVAILABLE FROM AMAZON AND KINDLE ISBN 978-1-78280-802-2

. . /

Charl Frock

After several decades of corporate slavery in a variety of industries and geographies, Charl has been working on producing a first fictional novel and a book of short stories, based loosely on some of his bizarre experiences encountered in corporate life across the globe. These works are a departure from his previous non-fiction publications in corporate literature.

Numbers

"I have just tickled a rat's genitals," my friend announces emphatically, as her call interrupts another gulp of my well-earned wine.

Flabbergasted, I put the glass down with such force I snap the stem but fortuitously manage to catch my newly-fashioned fishbowl before any of its precious contents spill out. Picking up my phone, dropped during the salvage operation, I can hear background noise and sense that she's waiting for reassurance that this sort of behaviour is normal, but I'm too preoccupied wondering whether her action carries a mandatory sentence.

Cradling the fishbowl in one hand, I reach for the bottle in the hope of exacting one last drop but know my efforts will be in vain. It's been a gruelling day at the office trying to prevent my department from becoming entrapped in millennial wokeness and I'd hoped copious quantities of wine would erase any recollection of the stressful and unproductive start to my week.

"What was that noise? You still there?" she asks.

I do not wish to be charged as an accomplice, not least, I'm uncertain whether she is talking about a human or the animal itself. Either way, the images flashing through my mind are deeply disturbing. Hanging up, leaving her to think I have keeled over in shock would be the most sensible option, but instead, filled with Dutch courage and resigned as accomplice to a rat molester, I dive right in. "Anyone I know?"

"Do you ever think of anything other than chasing tail?" she retorts.

Rather than state the bleeding obvious, I return the conversation to the lucky rat. "What did you tickle them with?"

"A tissue. It's quite easy when you know how."

I'm glad that I don't and contemplate whether alcohol is served to inmates.

She's eager to provide further context. "Chardonnay brought it in during the night. I woke to distressed squeaks coming from the bath where it was being subjected to a game of Gladiators. I couldn't bear to allow the inevitable conclusion and decided to separate captor and captive. Chardonnay protested vehemently at me removing him from his impromptu colosseum, but I eventually emerged victorious and put the little creature in a box in the garage to prevent its recapture. This morning, I was so surprised to see that it had survived its harrowing ordeal, I decided it would be best to rehome it. I drove it several miles into the countryside and after finding a secluded spot, was just about to introduce it to its new surroundings, when I noticed its eyes weren't open yet, so I scooped 'Numbers' back into the box and drove to work."

Better judgement clouded by my alcohol consumption I find the question "Why?" escaping my lips.

"It's called 'Numbers' because its aren't up yet," she pronounces. For the first time in my life, I yearn for an alarm clock to wake me.

"I mean, why did you take it to the office?"

"Because every creature deserves a fair chance." She clearly hasn't met any of the creatures I work with. I resist the temptation to say that I think leaving the cat to decide its fate was tantamount to giving Numbers, (may as well address it by name), a fair chance.

Numbers' introduction to the office caused a very mixed response. Nonetheless during the day, her very loyal and supportive team at the practice have apparently become experts in rat rearing – the four-legged kind. Not least, she informs me that after much Googling, she has learned how to distinguish a mouse from a rat, which has already come in handy as Numbers is unmistakeably the latter, not the former as she'd originally surmised. I find myself wishing I'd also developed a skill to distinguish rats from mice – the human kind.

Further forays into the internet by her team also revealed that baby rats require feeding every three hours for at least a month and that excreting is not instinctive. I'm still undecided whether the team member who plucked up the courage to inform her that after each feed, a rat's genitals must be tickled to make it urinate and poo, deserves a medal for bravery or rebuke for ensuring the addition of a rat to the client base of an extremely busy professional services firm.

"Rats are very social animals and build their nests close together," she continues. I do not have the courage,

Dutch or otherwise, to point out that Chardonnay has fortuitously stumbled upon a cat's version of online convenience shopping.

She takes several minutes to complete the Numbers narrative insisting she couldn't carry out the genital tickling sober. I can't disagree and am miffed that she has a genuine excuse to remain intoxicated for over a month. The long pauses as she gathers her thoughts while sipping on a vodka tonic mood stabiliser provide me with the opportunity to research how many diseases rats carry - at least seven according to the internet. I am struggling to warm to Numbers.

The conversation ends with her observation that I lack empathy for the hapless creature. I offer no resistance and peer into my empty fishbowl. Sadly, the Numbers narrative does not end here.

Predictably, Chardonnay wastes no time exploiting his good fortune and proudly returns from rat nest-pillaging with six more rat babies. Each arrival is announced by a call during the course of the night from my increasingly incoherent friend until she finally has the good sense to confine him. Certain after each call that my sleep will be interrupted by the next, I reflect soberly on my friend's candid observation, over several more fishbowls of wine. By morning, I reach the logical conclusion that after twenty years of corporate life, without an empathetic bone in my body, I'm unsuited to managing people.

POSTSCRIPT: Not all rat babies survived the night but after much genital tickling, Numbers, Letters and Emoji flourish thanks to their devoted team of highly qualified accountants.

Chardonnay remains under house arrest with no imminent possibility of parole.

Hilary McBride

26 November 1944 to 9 December 2014

Hilary was instrumental in developing IsleWrite, raising funds, welcoming speakers and recruiting indefatigably whenever the chance arose - Zumba classes included.

She moved to Thanet after a varied career in health education and became involved in a wide variety of charitable community initiatives.

Hilary wrote and published a novel *Dancing Round the Maypole*, co-writing with June Angliss a collection of short stories *Exactly the same but oh so different!* Many of Hilary's poems and short stories appeared in IsleWrite anthologies amongst others. The St Peter's Village Tour gave her another opportunity to shine and inspired her to write *The Diary of a Rat Catcher*.

A First Kiss

Her face was red with exertion, her hair limp with fronds stuck to her forehead.

Sweat trickled down her temples and between her breasts. Never had she worked so hard for so long. She glanced up at the clock on the wall. Nearly seven hours it had been... exhausting, painful hours.

All she wanted to do was close her eyes and sleep forever but everyone around was chattering excitedly, bustling here and there.

Her eyelids drooped, her muscles eased from tension to relaxation and she felt herself drift away. A tap on the shoulder brought her unwillingly to the here and now, wondering where she would find the strength to start all over again.

'This is what you've been waiting for,' said a voice close to her ear, slipping a small bundle into her arms.

She stretched out a finger to pull away the towelling and peered at the tiny, screwed-up purple face. Its two lips pursed in a butterfly-light kiss. A smile stretched across her face as her heart swelled with love for her new son.

Remember

What memories are secreted behind this ancient face of mellow weather-beaten rose?

The twinkling multi facets of her eyes look out onto an ever changing world.

Yet, inwardly, only she knows the truth of the past but cannot now reveal.

Her smiling open-mouthed façade welcomes friends, strangers and numerous visitors alike.

For over three hundred years this old house has listened, observed, wondered, suffered, and delighted in the myriad worlds of those who once lived within her walls.

Only when all her doors are shut fast, and the world outside is hushed does she stand, proud and strong.

Then, and only then, silently remembers.

Janette Mary Phethean

Janette is an artist, poet and author. She describes her writing as *painting pictures with words*. Born of Welsh parents, she is inspired by the land of music and verse, as she also composes music to some of her poems. Her work has been published in several anthologies and Janette gives credit and thanks to IsleWrite members for their continued support, encouragement and friendship.

Janette's poem *Remember* won a Pop-up Poetry competition sponsored by Jane Austen's House.

Jane Austen's House in Chawton, Hampshire is the picturesque country cottage where Jane Austen lived. It is the most treasured Austen site in the world. It was here that Jane's genius flourished and where she wrote, revised and had published all her major works: *Sense and Sensibility, Pride and Prejudice, Mansfield Park, Emma, Northanger Abbey* and *Persuasion.*

The house holds an important collection of objects associated with Jane Austen, including letters written by Jane and personal effects belonging to her and her family. Particular highlights include her jewellery and the table at which she wrote her much loved novels.

Jane Austen's House
Winchester Road, Chawton GU34 1SD
01420 83262
Charity No 1156458
janeaustens.house

Tessa Woodward

Tessa was a teacher, teacher trainer, and the Professional Development Co-ordinator at Hilderstone College, Broadstairs, Kent, until August 2016, and still edits *The Teacher Trainer*, a journal she founded 34 years ago! She is the author of many books and articles for language teachers and teacher trainers. Her book, *Teacher Development Over Time* (2018, Routledge), written with Kathleen Graves and Donald Freeman, was a finalist for the British Council ELTONS Innovations awards in 2019.

Tessa is now enjoying a switch to writing short stories.

Where we are

Personally, I wouldn't want to live in a town. People everywhere. Passing by, popping in. You'd have to look half-way decent all the time, just in case people saw you or popped in. And you'd have to behave.

Where we are, we can wear what we like… old things, dressing gowns, woolly hats, gloves, and scarves in the house in cold weather. It's cosy. Relaxed.

And, where we are, we can do what we like. So, if I come across, say, a couple of rotten tomatoes in the fridge or an apple that's gone bad in the bowl, I can just open my side door and fling them out, high enough so they sail over the hedge into the field next door. And I know that some creature, a mouse, a bird, will appreciate the throwings sooner or later. You couldn't do *that* in the town, now could you?

And where we are, we've got room to spread. Take recycling for example. We've got room for tall bins with black tops, blue tops, green tops. We've got room for crates and bags for collecting old newspapers and magazines. And again, if we're cooking, we can just open the side door and fling out an empty can onto the path. Next time we're outside, we can just take it round the back and pop it in a recycling bin.

Of course, if anything untoward happens in the country, you are pretty much on your own. If there was an intruder, for example, you probably wouldn't bother ringing the police. I mean, they'd probably go to the wrong village for starters cos there's three different villages in the area with very similar names. There's Oakstead, Oakstone and Oakham. Then they'd be an hour trying to find you along all the lanes. Which is why my husband keeps a baseball bat by the cooker. He reckons a good biff with that will discourage most people.

Where we are, you do hear some odd things at night mind. Sometimes it sounds like a woman is screaming her head off being murdered. That's probably either a fox having a good time or a fox that's got a rabbit, who is not having such a good time.

We hear owls too. But they just sound like owls.

So, it's a different sort of life really, where we are. I'll give you a for instance.

One chilly night last Autumn, it was dark and we'd got changed for bed early. The house was a bit chilly, so we'd got our woolly hats and scarves on. We were just finishing off the dinner dishes in the kitchen, when I heard a bit of a clattering by the side door.

'What's that?' I said.

'What?' said my husband.

. . >

There was another clatter.

'That!' I whispered.

My husband looked alert and walked quietly to the side of the cooker. He fished out his baseball bat. I switched the kitchen light off. We stood in the dark and listened.

More clattering and a bit of clanging, very close to the house. My husband walked to the side door and peered out its little window. But it was pitch black out there.

'Can't see anything,' he whispered.

He very quietly unlocked and opened the door. Lifting the baseball bat high above his shoulder, he stepped out smartly and shouted, 'Who the hell are you?'

Silence.

Nobody there.

He shouted again. Again nothing.

Right behind him, I then switched on the outside light so we could see the intruder. The path and the near part of the garden lit up. We looked around. It was silent. We could see nobody.

We waited, our dragon breath showing in the cold night air. Nothing.

Then, from somewhere near our feet there was a noise of metal on metal. We looked down.

A pilchard tin, one we'd thrown out in the middle of cooking, was moving around on its own, bumping into other tins, now empty of their plum tomatoes. Every time the pilchard tin hit another tin it made a metallic clang, stopped for a moment, backed up a bit, changed direction and then moved off again. The tin was being propelled by a stocky little body with prickles and a pair of skinny back legs. A hedgehog. Evidently attracted by the smell of fish, it had stuck its head inside the tin, greedy for the oil at the bottom. Head rammed in, the hedgehog had probably guzzled happily. But having finished its treat, it now found it couldn't get back out again. So there it was.

. . >

Head in tin, unable to see, body stuck, encased, the hedgehog was blundering around, only its back legs visible. Whenever it hit another tin with its pilchard tin helmet, the clang of metal was probably amplified enough to give the little creature inside a headache. So it would stop for a bit, wait for the sound to clear and then totter off again.

'Oh, for heaven's sake!' I said.

Clang! The pilchard tin had hit something. It backed up a bit, turned at an angle of about 45 degrees and staggered off to the edge of the path. There it bumped into the brick wall. It head butted the wall a few times.

Clang, clang, clang! The animal was getting desperate.

I bent over and grabbed the pilchard tin, holding it steady while the hedgehog struggled. Bracing itself, it gradually managed to back itself out.

'Well, look at you!' I said to the newly emerged hedgehog.

The creature's pointy face was slick with fish oil. Its prickles were smeared with bits of tomato. Blinking, huffing and puffing, the hedgehog looked a bit stunned. Then recovering somewhat, and probably still blinded by the outside light, it turned around and trundled off, blinking, into the shrubbery.

I looked at my husband. He was still holding his baseball bat aloft. We were both wearing dressing gowns and woolly hats. The path was littered with empty cans. Scattered about were a few rotten tomatoes and bad apples that we had tossed out the side door but which had failed to reach the necessary trajectory to make it over the hedge into the field next door. Altogether it made an odd scene.

'Just as well we didn't call the police.' I said.

No, I wouldn't want to live in a town.

TESSA'S FIRST COLLECTION OF STORIES, *TEN MINUTE TALES* (PLUS CD) WAS PUBLISHED IN 2019 AND INCLUDES *WHERE WE ARE* WHICH IS REPRINTED FROM THAT COLLECTION WITH PERMISSION

Donna Faber

Donna's childhood in Singapore ended in a desperate escape with her mother as the Japanese invasion began. Their perilous journey on the SS Narkunda and subsequent life in different parts of Australia formed the background of her novel *Child*. An excerpt was published in the *Daily Mail* on the anniversary of the ending of the War in the Far East.

Donna was a guiding light in IsleWrite's early days and her short stories featured in numerous anthologies. She now spends her time painting, with exhibitions around South-East England.

Chicken Soup

Ronnie's chopping celery – the way *she* likes it chopped. After that, it's carrots, onion, then raw chicken. Garlic he can do his way – *she's* never specified. And of course, Ronnie, don't forget the touch of lemon, will you? This is Sunday, his day of leisure, and he's making soup while Celeste lies upstairs flicking over magazine pages and his fishing gear is waiting for him.

    'Ronnie? Ronneeee?'

    He can hear the wheedling call from her bedroom - turns up the radio, scrapes the diced food into a large pan. It never used to be like this. Trouble is, used-to-bes are best not dwelt upon. Or maybes.

It was her Frenchness that first attracted him, twenty years ago. She'd come to learn English at a school in Westgate-on-Sea, stayed at his family home. His parents had thought her reserved - perhaps a little prudish for a Parisian – nice, though.

He smiles, remembering. That summer, he'd taken her fishing at Grove Ferry; she'd assured him, in her charming broken English, that she wouldn't be bored no, not at all. She wanted to share his hobbies. The grass was dry and turning yellow and they lay near the river bank watching a hawk. Celeste smelled alluring – was it jasmine or just her delicate skin? Afterwards, he realised that she'd had no intention of fishing and that, at least until the end of the summer, he wouldn't be doing any either.

By the end of her stay, his parents' opinion of Celeste had altered. 'Better watch it, Ron. She'll have you running around after her till you're in yer box. I've seen that type before,' said Dad.

'Shameless – those clothes she's wearing,' said Mum, 'hardly cover her essentials.'

He supposed that he hadn't really loved her, she was too withdrawn, too meticulous, not his type of girl. But lust thudded like a flash-flood through parched land, forcing rocks and trees before it. It swirled away the promptings of reason, the parents' mutterings. Fishing too was swept aside. They got engaged. She insisted.

Ronnie pours boiling water onto a stock cube and adds it to the pan. He wonders if John and the rest have caught anything. Noon already – damn! Most of the day gone and here he was, still dancing around for madame.

She's calling. He'd better go and see what's the matter *this* time. He trudges upstairs and stands in the doorway of her bedroom. 'What's up, then?'

'Ronnie, are you making the chicken-rice soup?' Celeste, propped against the pillows, lowers her glasses a fraction. 'The way I like it?'

'Yes.' He clenches the doorknob. 'Did

IMAGE - SANDWICH LAKES, KENT © DONNA FABER

. . >

you call me all the way up just to ask me that?'

'Don't get angry – I'm not asking much, am I? After all, I can't help being ill.' She pouts.

How could he once have thought that so enticing? 'What exactly is wrong with you, Celeste? It seems that you're spending more time than ever in bed.'

'I just feel bad inside, cheri. You wouldn't understand, you don't have women's problems.' Her voice as well as her words are hitting the note now – the level that makes him want to switch off, to run away, to gallop over the fields like the young roan near the carpark at Grove Ferry; to gallop and gallop and never come back.

'Perhaps you should see the doctor?' His voice is steady, even considerate, as he slips into the familiar role of puppet.

'And what could *he* do?' She whines, 'If we'd had children, cheri, maybe then I wouldn't be suffering with the menopause like I am. Or maybe if I had a more sympathetic husband…'

Ronnie shrugs. He wishes he could be different, but he can't. She's worn him down with years of pills and sighs. 'I'd better get on with the soup,' he says.

'Get me the little bell before you go, Ron, so I don't have to shout.' She strokes her throat. 'My voice, it's weakening.'

He turns the gas low under the pan, adds salt and pepper, looks at the clock. Nearly time to add the rice. As he's grating the lemon-rind, the phone rings.

'Whatya doin' mate? Thought you were allowed out today? Fish're swarming.' Ronnie can hear, in between his words, the murmur of the river, the dragonflies, the reeds moving in the current.

Celeste is ringing her bell.

'Just a minute, mate, I'll take this in the other room.' Ronnie shuts himself in the conservatory. 'Caught much, then?'

'I'll say. When are you coming?'

Ronnie closes his eyes, feels a silver body under his hand, smells it, throws it back. Fixes new bait, casts out again. 'I'm coming. Just held up a bit, that's all.' How can he explain about Celeste? It's all right for them, they've got their wives trained. 'See you later. Bye.'

He holds his hand to his nose – it doesn't smell of fish, only zest.

While the soup is simmering he goes into the garage to sort his gear. Stool, umbrella, rods, bag – he'll put them in the car now, before he takes up her lunch. He goes back for the bait - maggots.

Ronnie opens the jar – lovely little fellers, almost wriggling out the top with glee – he feels like he's ten years old.

The unanswered bell is ringing again, fainter now.

She's not going to spoil his day any more, he decides on the way back to the kitchen. He lifts the lid of the saucepan... Careful, I'll need some for fishing, he tells himself.

Wait till I tell the lads – later, when we're at the pub perhaps – get a few bevvies down first. They'll crease up.

He takes up her tray with the steaming dish, the crusty roll and butter, the napkin and the glass of Bordeaux. Maybe I've overdone it with the single rose – never mind – always did have a warped sense of humour, he tells himself.

It's hard wiping the smile off his face as he goes in and sets the tray down.

Celeste shakes out the napkin. 'Are you not joining me, cheri?'

'Not this time, love, I've already eaten.'

She dips the spoon into the soup. 'Oh! What is this? This is not rice.'

'Yes – a new kind, from the health-food shop.' He sits on the far side of the bed for a moment. 'Thought you'd enjoy that, instead.'

Resentment is draining away at the prospect of the afternoon ahead. He almost feels a twinge of guilt. Almost.

'But it is a very strange colour, is it not?'

'It's what they call unpolished,' he lies. 'Anyway, I'll leave you to it. There's things I want to do now.' He goes downstairs and locks the house, gets in his car.

As he reverses out of the drive, he can hear the bell, tinkling wildly through her open window.

. . /

Eric Charles Bartholomew

Eric Charles Bartholomew started writing when he was sixty (it's never too late), having worked in London and abroad for over forty years including five years lecturing in his chosen profession. Eric and his wife Mary enjoyed travel. Their first trip covered India, Sri Lanka and the Maldives. They fell in love with India and returned many times, eventually living there for several years. They have travelled extensively since, meeting fellow travellers, sharing their highs and lows, and swapping exaggerated stories over a glass or two of local brew.

Eric and Mary now live by the sea in Kent, retired in peace. But when the energy levels are up they still look for adventure and excitement.

Prologue

A figure pushed the bulkhead door open on its well-greased hinges, the light from behind silhouetting his dark torso. He moved silently, closing the steel door behind him and stepped quickly to the side of the great ship. He tossed a life jacket over the side. As it hit the water, a yellow light came on automatically flashing its mayday signal - on, off, on, off. Suddenly he caught the sound of waterproof clothing rustling somewhere in the dark. He stood stock still, not daring to breathe. The glow from an inhaled cigarette illuminated a shape skulking in the corner of a bulkhead and briefly lit up rusty steel walls and paint-peeled rivets. The black ship throbbed forward, the steel floor vibrating under them.He moved stealthily forward, smiling to himself. It was one of the midnight watches.

As his eyes became accustomed to the darkness, he made out the outline of the figure standing in the corner. The glow from the cigarette died and the man at the bulkhead turned, spotted the flashing light and raised his arm automatically.

'Man over - '. No other sound left his lips. The hilt of a knife stuck out from his throat; the long steel blade had severed his windpipe. Blood and mucus dribbled from his lips, splashing onto his waterproof coat. He slumped forward.

The black figure took his weight easily. Dragging the dying man towards the ship's side, he slid him over the gunnels. The body dropped like a stone, hitting the surface with a great splash. The dark figure looked around. No-one had seen or heard a thing. He smiled to himself once more...

ERIC'S NOVEL *DISTANT HORIZONS* WAS FIRST PUBLISHED IN GREAT BRITIAN IN 2009 BY KAVANAGH TIPPING PUBLISHING, ISBN: 13: 978-1906546052. ALSO BY ERIC *ANGELS AND DIRTY FACES* THE STORY OF AN IRASCIBLE BOY IN THE EAST END STREETS OF THE 1950s. ERIC CAN BE CONTACTED AT *ERICBARTHOLOMEW95@GMAIL.COM*

IsleWrite...

In the closing years of the last millennium, the University of Kent offered a creative writing course at Hilderstone College in Broadstairs, led by the inspirational Maggie Solley.

Members of that class were so motivated that they re-enrolled for another year - and then another. Eventually, it was politely pointed out that they were blocking places which could be taken by other aspiring writers.

Undeterred, the group decided to meet initially as *The Biscuit Club* – there were always biscuits – and then as IsleWrite (I'll write) because that's what each was determined to do.

Based on the Isle of Thanet – glorious, history-redolent and more than slightly special – IsleWrite is a group supporting writers from all walks of life, many from other countries who have found their way to Kent. Some have written from an early age, others are early in their writing journey. Some write fiction – short stories, novels and plays; some write memoir; others prefer poetry. Each has a story to tell and individual successes are celebrated by all. In addition to sharing work, the group hosts guest speakers, conducts workshops and runs writing competitions.

With works by thirty writers, **twentythirty** celebrates the first twenty years of IsleWrite.

islewrite.co.uk

 IsleWrite

 # Isle Write Twenty Thirty